THE LAST LOVE STORY

A Baker Girls Romance

BETHANY MONACO SMITH

For more information about this book, visit the author's website.
www.bethanymonacosmith.com

Editing by Lacey Braziel of On the Page Publishing
Cover Design by Chelsea Kemp
Formatting by Bethany Monaco Smith

ABOUT THE LAST LOVE STORY

The Last Love Story is the third book in the Baker Girls interconnected standalone series. All books in the series can be read as standalone novels.
The Last Love Story is a low angst, marriage of convenience rom-com featuring plus-size romance author Jade Jackson and swoony romance narrator and cover model Justin Ayers. *The Last Love Story* is full of flirting, tension, banter, some forced proximity, and plenty of swoony and steamy moments.
Ready to fall in love with Jade & Justin?

MEET THE CHARACTERS

The romance lovebirds:
Jade Jackson
Justin Ayers

The Baker Girls crew:
Frannie Baker
Kennedy Baker
Hallie Baker
Devon McGregor
Ryan "Hardy" Hardison
Brian Ackley
Mark Abbott

Jade's family/friends:
Jade's dad (aka Papa Jackson)
Trish Davies
Zoey Holloway

TRIGGER WARNINGS

If you're looking for possible triggers in this book, this page is for you. If you're not, you can skip this page and dive into the story.

trigger warnings may contain plot spoilers

As a lighthearted read, I tried my best to keep this one as trigger-free as possible. However, this book does feature a predatory male in the romance space. The FMC is on the receiving end of brief unwanted physical contact from him (his hand on her butt). This is short-lived and not heavily discussed. Other briefly mentioned possible triggers: fatphobia/ fat shaming, homophobia/transphobia & general bigotry.

Any updates or changes to this information can be found at bethanymonacosmith.com/triggers

To anyone who looks into the mirror and doesn't love what they see, I see you. Give yourself the same love and grace you'd give the most important people in your life. You're worthy of it.

CHAPTER ONE

Justin

LISTENING to your best friends bang isn't all it's cracked up to be.

I'm grateful I've had a couple of weeks to spend with Devon and Kennedy. We don't get to see each other nearly enough being in different parts of the country for the last few years. And I'm thrilled they *finally* realized their feelings for each other and are happily together after being complete idiots for most of their lives. I just wish the spare room didn't share a wall with their bedroom.

Guess it's back to reading for me. What better way to spend the next hour?

Even if they don't fuck for that long, they'll be busy for that long. And while I could go out and roam around the small suburb they live in, I don't have any connection to the area. It's another town that doesn't feel like home.

I'm starting to wonder if anywhere ever will.

That train of thought can go fuck itself because the last thing I need is to be depressed while my friends put on a show in the background.

Grabbing my wireless earbuds and my e-reader, I get comfortable in the oversized chair by the window and get back to my latest binge.

I'm not one to complain about some extra time to read, especially when the series I'm reading has lodged itself in my brain the way this one has. I started it on the plane out to California from Georgia, and I'm already on book six. This author has several other long-running series, and I have a feeling her books are going to be all I read for the next few weeks.

I'm not ashamed to admit I'm a sucker for a romance novel. They're an essential part of my life as both a voice actor and a model—known for romance novel covers and narration now. I love a good love story, and I always have. As a kid, I had to hide that from my dad—the fun of misogyny—but now I flaunt it. It's a part of me I never want to hide. Some of the best books I've ever read have been romance novels, and my favorites tackle far more than love. Whether it's societal issues, mental health, or family dynamics, I love getting into the nitty gritty with characters.

The current author I'm reading—Jade Jackson—is incredible at knitting everything together. She also writes long-running series that have a real-life feel and doesn't shy away from topics that some people are more afraid of in the romance genre, like cheating and how a relationship can either be broken or heal afterward. I don't know which way it'll go for this couple, but I'm desperate to find out. Even though there's only one more book out in this series so far, and I don't think their storyline has been resolved yet.

I find my playlist of reading music and put it on, then think twice and head to the author's social media, hoping I'll find links for audiobooks. I love to listen along while I read, but when I searched in one of the bigger apps for audiobooks, I couldn't find any for this series, which surprised me. I've been seeing it pop up a lot.

I scroll through her social media, which has a perfect aesthetic vibe with pictures of her books or things that inspire her. Noting a pinned post with FAQs, I click on it. On the third slide, she notes that, while she has audiobooks for one of her previous series, she doesn't have any audiobooks for this series because she's saving up to do them all at once. She wants to release them close together so people who depend on audio don't get stuck with cliffhangers for too long.

I love that she's thinking about that, but it sucks she doesn't have that financial freedom. As a narrator, I stand firm behind the prices I and my fellow narrators charge, but I'm also well aware how big of an investment that is for an author, and I wish there was a way to make it more affordable for authors and still get paid. There should be loans or grants tailored for authors like there are other small businesses. They deserve to have those opportunities too.

The selfish side of me wants these books in audio, and for a hot second, I wonder how ridiculous it would be for me to offer to record these for her with a royalty-share agreement. I could do it in my spare time. But she might see that as charity.

I need to let this go and just enjoy the story, but before I can navigate away from her page, I catch the pinned "about me" post and click on it. The second slide features a picture of her smiling as she sits on the floor, surrounded by piles of her books.

I stare at it for a moment, then zoom in, getting a better look at her. She's absolutely gorgeous. Curves everywhere and a smile that's so captivating I don't want to look away. Her hair is a deep brown that's almost black and done in soft waves. I blink a few times before I finally swipe to the next slide.

Then I scroll back and look at the picture again, something inside me firing up.

I don't exactly have a type. Not in terms of looks.

I'll fully admit, I'm a manslut sometimes.

I'm not going to apologize for it, though. I love women—everything about them. Every size, every shape.

While I don't indiscriminately sleep around, I also hook up a decent amount.

Not because I'm afraid of falling in love or catching feelings or anything else. I *wish* I would. But most of the time, it's a passing night with someone who is fine but I don't have a connection with besides the physical.

Like finding a town that feels like home, one day I want to find the right person to settle down and share my life with. I'm open to it right this second if they randomly walk through the door, but I know that's unlikely.

I've always loved reading and watching love stories. Someday, I hope I get to live my own.

Until then, it's back to reading them and living vicariously.

KENNEDY BREEZES past me where I'm sitting at the kitchen island, a mug in her hand, looking pointedly at me as she hums something. It takes me a second to figure out what it is.

Belle from *Beauty and the Beast.*

"Are you implying something?"

She spins to face me with a wide smile. "Not at all," she says innocently.

"Mhm."

"Just saying you've had your *nose stuck in a book* a lot."

I close my e-reader and pin her with a look.

"Only because Devon has had his"—I clear my throat—"stuck in your—"

She smacks me hard on the shoulder. "Asshole."

"Don't act like it's not true."

Her face falls for a second. "Sorry."

"It's fine, Kend. I'm happy you two are finally together. Plus, it gives me time to binge this series."

"Is that the author you were talking about having you by the balls when you got here?" Devon asks as he strolls into the room.

"Maybe." I'm hesitant to say that now. Since I saw her picture, something about that seems pervy. Knowing she's hot as fuck and created this rich world to fall in love with is doing something to me.

Something I need to let go of.

"Who is it?" Kennedy asks. She loves romance books *almost* as much as I do.

"Jade Jackson."

"Oh, I've heard of her, but I haven't read anything." She grins at me. "Tell me where to start."

"I'll text you."

"Noooo," Devon fake complains. "I finally got you, and now I'm going to lose you to a book series?"

Kend tips her head. "You could read it with me."

"Oh, highly recommend," I tell him. "I mean I haven't gotten to do that yet, but reading spicy books with a partner? Why wouldn't you?"

Devon blinks at me, then turns to Kennedy, eyes predatory.

"I could get behind that."

He grabs her face and leans down to kiss her.

"And back to reading."

"No. Stop." Kennedy steps away from Devon. "It's our last night here before we head to New York tomorrow. Let's do something fun. Order in a bunch of takeout and be dumbasses like we used to. Or we can go out for dinner. Karaoke?" She shimmies her shoulders. "What do you think?"

"I'm in," Dev says.

I glance back at the e-reader. I *really* want to know what happens next, but I guess I can wait and hang out with my friends. Odds are they'll be fucking like rabbits later tonight anyway.

"Yeah. Sounds good."

I stand up, but as I walk toward the stairs, I pull out my

phone, pull up Jade's profile again, and hit follow. Might as well build a connection now since I'll probably be president of her fan club this time next month.

CHAPTER TWO

Jade

I WHEEZE for a breath as I snort-laugh into my wineglass.

It's possible I've had too much to drink.

My friends, Zoey and Trish, are doing the exact same thing, though. So either we've all had too much to drink or I should open another bottle because we're still coherent enough to tell stories that make us laugh like hyenas.

Zoey's was something about her douche-husband. No. Ex-douche. No. Her ex-husband who is a flaming douche. With all the bells and whistles, including misogyny and homophobia.

I never really met him other than in passing, but the way she describes him paints the only picture I need. That tracks, though, since like me, Zoey is also a romance author.

We were lucky enough to connect when a bookstore had a signing for local authors a few years back. She lives in the neighboring town of Lacy Creek, which is slightly bigger than my tiny two-stoplight town of Woods Junction.

It's an adorable little town, and the inspiration for the towns in many of my stories.

I glance at my phone, then resist the urge to check on my sales and how much money I've made today. I'm trying to break the habit of checking daily now that I have a more consistent success and income level, but it's hard not to. It took years and my backlist grew a lot faster than my income, but I've found better ways to promote my niche stories lately, and over the last year am making a full-time income, but barely. Once I factor in paying for my own health insurance and all my business costs, I'm still low income, but I'm so much happier than I was when I was working full or part time doing anything else. It's just trickier to invest in my business how I want to right now, but I'm hoping as I continue to grow, it'll get easier.

I pull my hand back. *I'm not going to check.* But then my phone goes off, and... was it listening?

I snag it off the table, but what I find is not some magical report on my sales, but a bunch of social media notifications. I go to swipe them all away, but freeze with my thumb above one of the notifications.

"Oh my god," I squeak.

Zoey and Trish are immediately at attention.

"What is it?" Zoey asks. "Did someone tag you in something mean? I'll cut them."

I laugh at that, but it comes out more nervous than playful. "No. It's, ah... Justin Ayers followed me."

Trish drops her phone. "Justin Ayers. Like the super-hot cover model and new favorite romance narrator?"

"Yep."

"Well, was it a follow back? Like you followed him? He might like supporting authors."

He has over three hundred thousand followers. Somehow, I doubt he follows back every author who follows him. Plus... "I'm not following him."

Trish's brows fly up. "You're not? But why? I know you love at least five books he's narrated."

"Yes, but I don't... know him."

Zoey laughs a little at this. She gets it more than Trish does. Sometimes you choose not to follow certain people because you don't want to look like you're desperate or trying to get something or another fangirl.

Or, in my case, because I might have a stupid parasocial crush on him. It's totally ridiculous. We've never met. The only reason I have a crush on him is because his voice makes me melt. Sure, he's hot too. Tall, blond, and ripped with stunning blue eyes. But that's not what really matters. Either way, it's ridiculous. Having a crush on someone you don't actually know is a recipe for disaster. For all I know, he might be a total asshole in real life. I don't actually know him. So I didn't follow him.

Trish leans in, whispering like the walls might have ears. "Wait. Do you actually know Pedro Pascal and Taylor Swift? Have you been holding out on us?" She gives me a mischievous smirk. While she can pretend to be the idiot, she's probably the smartest of the three of us. She works as a college librarian and is all brainy bookworm with the looks of a model. Some people are truly blessed.

No.

Being thin is not the ideal body shape, no matter what the world says. Trish is gorgeous, but so is Zoey, who, like me, is curvy or plus size or fat or whatever the correct term is—whatever one is used to make people comfy or that was once bad and we've taken back. I'm the biggest of the three of us, and though I'd like to say I never think about that, I obviously do. It's not that I want to. I'm working on healing from my body image issues, and I've come a long way. For the first time in my life, I have a lot of peace about my body and truly see myself as beautiful. But that doesn't stop the negative thoughts from filtering in, and sometimes I have to sit with them for a few minutes before I can shut them down and move on.

It's an old habit to assume anyone who looks pretty has it all, when I know well enough that Trish doesn't. As amazing as she is, she's a real human, and I don't want to give in to the comparison shit, especially with my friends.

Okay, mini meltdown over.

"Should I follow him back now?"

"Do you want to?" Zoey asks.

I wanted to before, but again, I didn't want to do the parasocial creepy crush thing. But if he followed me first, that negates it, right? I'm following back because I enjoy his work and he followed me. We're in the same industry, we can support each other.

"Yes," I say, then click the button.

And as soon as I do, another notification pops up.

A message. From him. It must have been in my requests.

"Oh my *god*."

"What?" Zoey yells, crawling over the couch to me.

"He sent me a message."

"Open it!" Trish shrieks.

I quickly go to his profile, double checking it's not a scam.

No. It's really him. Which means... Justin Ayers really sent *me* a message.

Okay, be cool.

Navigating over to my messages, I open them and find several in a row from Justin.

JUSTIN AYERS

Hey, Jade. This might come off totally random, but I'm reading your Mariano Family series, and I'm… a little obsessed. With your writing. Not trying to be pervy in your inbox, I swear. I just wanted to tell you how amazing it is. I know I'm falling into your world ass backward and there's a bunch of series I'll need to catch up on when I finish this one, but once I started, I couldn't stop. You've got me in a chokehold. I just started the seventh book, and I'm just curious how far you are on the eighth?

JUSTIN AYERS

Okay, now I sound creepy again. Let me start over…

JUSTIN AYERS

Hi, Jade. I've become a huge fan of your writing, and I know how hard this industry is, so I just wanted to let you know that. I can't wait to read more.

JUSTIN AYERS

Does your fan club have a president? Because I volunteer as tribute.

JUSTIN AYERS

And now that I've thoroughly embarrassed myself, I'm going to go. Feel free to message me back… if this doesn't make you block me. Okay. Bye.

I blink at my phone in disbelief. That is not what I was expecting.

Trish paws at my leg. "What does it say?"

"He's reading the Mariano Family series, and he's loving it."

Trish squeaks and claps her hands.

"That's amazing," Zoey says. "And he should be loving it because that series is incredible. I'm glad I get to read book eight before everyone else," she teases.

"He asked when it was going to be done... oh my gosh. This is crazy."

"Maybe you should ask him to narrate it," Trish says.

"Like I could afford him. And I'm not going to use his love of the series to my advantage. That's not cool."

"Fine," Trish says as I set my phone to the side. "You're not going to respond to him?"

"Not right now. This is girl time." Plus, I need to be alone to figure out what to say without the writing and reading devils in my ears. They'd be suggesting I send direct lines from my books.

We've definitely had enough wine.

"Let her be," Zoey says with a laugh.

"As long as we get details," Trish says.

"You're nosy," Zoey says, shoving Trish's arm.

"Obviously. Have you not met me? Meddling is fun."

Zoey gives a long-suffering sigh. She's probably been on the receiving end of that more than anyone. They've been besties since they were kids, and with Trish now engaged to their other friend Mikey, she's been a little extra pushy about Zoey's feelings for Mikey's brother Luke. Zoey swears up and down they're just friends, but they definitely aren't. It's fun watching your friends live out real-life romance tropes.

I glance back at my phone. Is there a romance trope waiting for me?

Nope. I am not going there. Not at all.

There's a loud knock on my door, and Trish grabs her phone. "Must be the warden."

"I can hear you," Mikey says through the door.

We dissolve into a fit of giggles, and Mikey swings the door open. Scanning the coffee table, he sighs. "How much wine have you had?"

I shrug innocently. "Those were empty when we got here. It's magic."

"Uh huh. Good thing I brought reinforcements." Then Luke

walks in behind him, all long-ish hair and tattoos. Zoey practically purrs when she sees him. But sure, no feelings there.

"Have they been getting into trouble?"

"We're innocent angels, *thank you*," Zoey says to Luke.

The predatory smile on his face is downright indecent.

Mikey glances at me, as if thanking me now for getting them a little tipsy, like he hopes that'll push Zoey and Luke over the edge.

I shake my head and climb off the couch, then make sure Trish and Zoey have everything.

Mikey wraps a big arm around Trish and guides her out the door. Luke looks at Zoey. "You okay to walk by yourself?"

"Yes. I'm a big girl. I'm fine."

But I don't miss the way she leans into his hand on her back as I shut and lock the door behind them.

My eyes are heavy, and I'm surprisingly relaxed, if a little energized after reading that message from Justin.

Grabbing my water bottle and phone, I switch off the lights, then head down the hall of my apartment to my bedroom.

Once I've washed my face, brushed my teeth, and put on my comfiest sleep clothes, I crawl into my bed and use the app on my phone to turn the air conditioner down another degree. I'd rather sleep cold than hot.

Then, because I can't help myself, I grab my phone and open those messages from Justin again.

Thanks for your message. It always feels amazing when someone says they love my books. For the record, I'm a fan of yours too. And sorry, the fan club president position is taken by a rabid reader friend, but I can see if she's willing to have a co-president.

JUSTIN AYERS

I'll get pom-poms and be your cheerleader. I'm just happy to shout about your books. Which I'll be doing the second I finish this book. Which will probably be tonight because I have no chill.

I love that for you, though you might hate that for yourself in the morning! I've stayed up late bingeing books a few too many times. It always hurts the next day.

JUSTIN AYERS

But the pain is worth it. Especially for this. I NEED to know what happens with Colby and Jess.

I send him one of those emojis that convey an uh-oh vibe. Because it's possible that's what this book's cliffhanger revolves around.

JUSTIN AYERS

You're killing me! Now I have to finish it. I need to know what happens.

If you survive the night, feel free to message me in the morning and tell me your feelings.

JUSTIN AYERS

You're leaving me to face this alone?

I don't know where you are, but it's almost midnight here. I like sleep. But feel free to rage message me. I won't see it until the morning anyway. 😏

JUSTIN AYERS

You're mean. That's mean.

You chose your path. Now you have to live with it. Have a good night.

JUSTIN AYERS

Somehow I get the feeling… I'm going to be in pain.

Don't say I didn't warn you…

[Taylor Swift Blank Space Gif]

JUSTIN AYERS

Is this going to hurt more or less than the ATWTMV?

Ha! I'm not sure, but I would highly suggest that song as a reading companion. Good night!

JUSTIN AYERS

Enjoy sleeping peacefully while I suffer.

Gotta be up early for my tea with the devil. 😌 Sweet dreams!

I laugh as I put my phone in do not disturb mode and turn out the light.

Maybe it's a good thing he messaged me. Now I can get to know the real person, and hopefully my unrealistic crush will fade.

CHAPTER THREE

Jade

"SURGERY IS THE BEST OPTION," my doctor says, dashing any remaining threads of hope I had about avoiding it.

Carpal tunnel is the worst, and mine has proved to be a particularly bad case. I've battled it for years, but over the last six months, it's gotten so severe that it's been much harder than normal for me to write or do a lot of basic tasks without pain.

My doctor warned me this was coming, but we were exhausting every other option—and lots of physical therapy first. But nothing helped. I even worked with an occupational therapist to set up my workspace and watch how I held my arms while I typed, but she was impressed with how much thought and attention I already put into it.

I tried switching to dictation, but it was difficult for me to write that way, and even when I did get some good content, the more frequent moving of the mouse to fix problem spots was even worse on my hand than typing.

It's only on my right side, so I try to rely on my left more, especially for everything not typing related, but there's only so much I can do since my right side is my dominant side.

I've done all I can do. Now... *fuck*. This is going to mess with everything. It will set back my writing schedule for the rest of the year unless I get a lot better at dictation.

"What does the recovery period look like?"

"It will probably take a couple of months to get back to normal for daily activities, and to fully restore hand strength can take between six months to a year. After the surgery, you'll start with rest and then move on to physical therapy."

"And how long before I can type again?" My voice is meek. I hate it. But it's like the center of my life is slipping away from me.

"As much as you are currently? Probably two to three months. You can ease into it sooner, but building up to it and maintaining good posture is going to be important."

"Okay. Thank you."

"Of course. I'll take you out to our receptionist so she can get you scheduled."

I swallow and nod, following him out of the room and down the hall until I'm sitting in an uncomfortable chair in front of a perpetually upbeat woman.

"Carpal tunnel release surgeries take place in our outpatient surgery area. You'll be awake for the surgery, and only a local anesthetic will be used." She slides a piece of paper across the counter between us. "This goes into further detail about it, and a nurse will call you forty-eight hours beforehand to discuss the details and preparation. It looks like we're scheduling a couple weeks out. I'm looking at June 29th."

"Um, I can't do that. I have to be out of town for work that weekend."

"Okay, our next availability is July 8th."

Nodding, I force a smile. "Yes. That should be fine."

"Great. We'll send everything along to your insurance company for prior approval. Sometimes they need to see proof you've tried other alternatives before they agree to pay for it. If that's the case, just give us a call and we can send them more paperwork."

"I can do that. Thanks."

"Have a good day."

Pushing out of the chair, I make my way toward the waiting room where my dad is sitting. He insisted on driving me so I don't stress my wrist out more.

He stands when he sees me, always moving a little slow when he first stands up. His brow furrows.

"What did he say?"

"Surgery."

"Sweetheart—"

I wave my hand, stopping his words. "Not here."

He nods in understanding, but rests his hand soothingly on my upper back as we walk toward the elevator.

Once we're safely out of the hospital and back in his car, tears burn in my eyes.

It's probably going to be fine, but I'm terrified it won't be. I'm terrified this will derail me when I'm finally on track. I'm continuously growing. And I almost have enough saved up to start audiobooks for the Mariano series. Hopefully, I can keep growing and record more of my backlist from there. But if my income starts crashing and I can't release more books?

I bury my face in my hands as I cry. All this is threatening a part of who I am. Maybe that's ridiculous. Plenty of people have successful careers with much worse situations than what I'm in. I know that. But I have to feel my emotions and let them out or they'll eat away at me.

"Hey, we're going to get through this," Dad says gently. "We've gotten through worse. Remember the time we got stranded in that tiny cabin in the woods because a tree fell over the road, then we both ended up with a stomach virus and had to share that tiny pot of a toilet?"

I sit up, laughing through my tears. "You went outside one time because you couldn't wait."

"And it was pouring."

His deep brown eyes, that are just like mine, twinkle with mischief.

"Thanks, Dad."

"It's going to be okay, sweetheart. What do you say? Brunch before we head home? We can go to that café you like."

I smile at that. "Sounds perfect. I need all the comfort food."

AFTER A NICE BRUNCH with my dad, I'm lounging on the couch, catching up on the latest season of my guiltiest pleasure, *Virgin River*. It's not a guilty pleasure because it's aimed toward women or because it's drama and romance heavy. Nope. References to those things as guilty pleasures can be left in the past. It's my guilty pleasure simply because it's so *messy*. Sometimes not in a good way. But I'm addicted, and I can't look away.

Tomorrow I'll finish the final chapter of book eight and write the delicious cliffhanger I've been waiting to type for three books now.

Part of me wants to write it today, but I'm tired. My hand is already tingling without doing much, and I want to pout and wallow. Tomorrow I'll get back at it, then I'll start my read through —and take a serious look at my schedule and how I think it's going to be affected by my surgery. There's no way I can comfortably bang out book nine beforehand, especially with my hand so sensitive.

Maybe I'll wait to start it... even though that might kill me.

I'm about to spiral down a rabbit hole of dictation software when my stomach rumbles.

If I'm going to doom research things, it's better to have coffee and some of my dad's homemade chocolate chip banana bread while I do.

I head for the kitchen and get my little comfort snack before returning to the couch.

All it takes is one delicious bite of the banana bread to improve my mood a little.

My dad is a great cook—so great he runs his own YouTube channel teaching people how to cook simple but comforting meals. He does it alongside his part-time job as an accessibility consultant to contracting companies.

My dad worked in the contracting industry for years until he was involved in a forklift accident that left him with chronic pain and some limited mobility in his left leg. He took all that and turned around and became an accessibility consultant. My dad has never been one to let life get him down, and he's a big part of the reason I chased my dream as an author.

I was still in college when I came home upset because another agent had rejected me without even laying eyes on my manuscript. I knew my stories were good, but getting it in front of an agent who thought it had potential wasn't happening. My dad asked why I couldn't just publish it myself. I didn't have an answer.

The next morning, I woke up to find a pile research about how to self-publish and three books about it on the way.

My dad is my fiercest supporter and my best friend. He's primarily the one who raised me, since he and my mom split when I was young. My mom is the type to wander around the world with a new guy every six months to a year. She's happy that way. At least, I think she is. There's no animosity between us, but we're not close. She's obsessed with the newest beauty standards and the wellness lifestyle, and that's not me. Don't get me wrong, I like taking care of myself, but my mom's version of that and mine are two different things. Dad always told me to let her live her life and for me to live mine in whatever way felt best.

I see my mom a couple of times a year, and it's all very relaxed, but she's more like a random relative than my mom, and I'm okay with that. It's better than trying to force a relationship that would never work.

After years of the single life, my dad is dating someone now, and I hope they end up together because I really like her.

Another bite of heavenly banana bread, and I decide not to go down any rabbit holes right now. It'll only stress me out. When I'm calmer, I can look into it all.

I send my dad a thank you text, and before I can put my phone down, it vibrates in my hand. I can barely contain my slightly chaotic smile when I see a message from Justin.

JUSTIN AYERS

I'm suing you for emotional damage.

I'm surprised it took you this long to message me. After our conversation last night, I was expecting to wake up to a string of messages cursing me out. But instead, I got crickets. I almost wondered if I made you so mad you blocked me. Not sure if that's a good or bad thing...

JUSTIN AYERS

You mock my pain. I ugly cried.

He sends a GIF of Jess Day from *New Girl* ugly crying.

JUSTIN AYERS

Live footage of me reading that last night. You ripped my heart out, then did an Irish jig on top of it.

An Irish jig? That's very specific.

JUSTIN AYERS

Are you enjoying my pain?

What kind of author would I be if I didn't like the fact that my words elicit such strong emotion?

JUSTIN AYERS

A human one. One with a soul.

I laugh as I take another bite of banana bread.

Hey, my soul hurts when I hurt my characters. I cry along with them. Then I smile when I watch my readers cry.

JUSTIN AYERS

Sadist.

Aw, thanks.

JUSTIN AYERS

Are you having tea with Satan right now?

Nope. That was this morning. Just coffee and some delicious banana bread.

JUSTIN AYERS

Good, I hope you're comfortable so you can listen to me complain about my emotional devastation for my whole flight.

Where are you headed?

JUSTIN AYERS

New York City for a modeling job.

Book cover?

JUSTIN AYERS

Nope, just an advertising gig. Some kind of cologne I'll never wear.

Well, if you can't stop crying about my books, you can pretend it's just the smell of the cologne.

JUSTIN AYERS

Has anyone ever mentioned you might have psychopathic tendencies?

> Only my therapist, but once I locked him in the basement, he stopped saying that.

JUSTIN AYERS

Do you secretly write thrillers?

> Ha. No. Just typing that felt weird. If it's not squishy and romantic, I don't want it.

JUSTIN AYERS

Fair enough. *Dramatic sigh* I guess I'll have to start another series to pass the time.

> ... one of mine?

JUSTIN AYERS

Because I'm a masochist... yes.

> At least all those are completed. They might break your heart, but they'll also come back and patch up all the cracks.

JUSTIN AYERS

That might be why I'm obsessed with your writing.

Ugh. I wish he wouldn't say things like that. It makes it hard to let go of this crush. Or more like it's hard for a new crush not to start. We've only had two conversations, but this time it's not a nonsense feeling I'm getting from hearing his voice. The little uptick in my heartbeat is because I like his playful nature, openness about his emotions, and the kindness I feel in the subtext of it all.

It's almost like... he's one of my book boyfriends.

Oh my god. Did I write him and bring him to life? Oh, that would be such a good plot for a 2000s Disney Channel Movie.

Or a book.

I mentally add it to my never-ending ideas folder and tuck it away for later.

All jokes aside, thanks for reading. I'm glad you're enjoying my books… even if you're clearly a sucker for heartache.

JUSTIN AYERS

I'm in for the long haul now. Is it cool if I keep messaging you stuff about them?

Absolutely. Fire away. If I'm in the middle of working, I usually put my phone in do not disturb mode, but I'll happily respond when I'm done. Which is how tomorrow will probably go since I have every intention of finishing book eight.

JUSTIN AYERS

Put your phone on do not disturb. Ignore me. Ignore everyone. Get your groceries delivered. I NEED to know what happens next.

Thanks for that. Have a good flight.

JUSTIN AYERS

Thanks. Time to get lost in some more of your torment. Have a good rest of the day.

With that, I set my phone down and look back at the TV, but my mind keeps wandering, planning out the specifics of the chapter I'll be writing tomorrow.

This one will have a cliffhanger, it won't be as big as book seven's was. Plus, it'll feature a different couple in the crossfire. Figuratively, not literally. I don't write action books or thrillers. Only books that break you into pieces before putting you back together.

Pausing the TV, I pick up my phone again, put it in do not disturb mode, then record a voice note. I can record voice notes all day. They're just my rambly thoughts about where I want a scene to go and occasionally a few lines of dialogue.

Dictation is much harder, as I have to both speak clearly and know exactly what I want to say. Often, I find the exact words while I'm typing, and I struggle to do that with dictation.

After a couple of long voice notes, I flip to my calendar and look through my writing schedule. I'll have to adjust things. But not book eight. I'll finish this one and then see where things go. Maybe over the next couple of weeks I can get ahead on stuff for my subscription service, so I won't be behind there. Only time will tell.

But enough of that. I'm supposed to be relaxing. My banana bread is gone, but I still have coffee left, so I hit play on the TV, then turn off do not disturb mode on my phone and scroll through my messages from Justin, which immediately bring a smile to my face.

JUSTIN AYERS

Okay, I started the Legal Love series. And really? Just casually decimating my heart in the first two chapters?

JUSTIN AYERS

I don't know if I love you or hate you.

JUSTIN AYERS

I'm already addicted to this book.

JUSTIN AYERS

I'm not sure if I love or hate the male main character. He just shows up, like hey, surprise! And she's supposed to just fall into his arms?

JUSTIN AYERS

I rescind my previous statement. I'm on his team now. Someone get me a T-shirt.

JUSTIN AYERS

Taking the "time left in the book" estimation as a personal challenge.

Glad you're enjoying yourself.

JUSTIN AYERS

What are you doing?

Watching Virgin River and relaxing.

JUSTIN AYERS

And plotting?

You already know me so well.

JUSTIN AYERS

I'd say we're soul mates, but I don't think soul mates are supposed to enjoy emotionally destroying each other.

What can I say? I'm special.

JUSTIN AYERS

Something like that. Anyway, I can't message and read at the same time, and I'm determined to finish reading this before my flight lands.

Good luck.

He sends me a saluting emoji, and I laugh as I lean back against the couch.

Now it's time to rest. If my brain will stop shouting ideas at me for long enough to do that.

CHAPTER FOUR

Justin

"DUDE, should I be getting you coffee instead of beer?" Devon asks as he slides a bottle in front of me, then sits down next to me in the semicircle booth at our old hangout spot in New York City.

"I wouldn't complain."

"You stayed up all night reading, didn't you?" Kennedy teases.

She and Dev flew out to New York on the same flight as me. While I have a job, they're here to finish packing Kennedy's apartment since she's moving in with Devon.

"I had to finish," I whine. *Then start another book on the flight*. It's not my fault that Jade's books are infused with some kind of magic that makes stopping impossible.

"Aw, is someone getting old? Can't pull all-nighters anymore?" Kennedy's cousin Hallie teases.

She's the youngest of the bunch at twenty-three. I give her the middle finger, and she laughs loudly. She was thirteen when I first met her, and was seventeen when I moved here after college with Devon and Kend, and we have a very sibling-like relationship.

The whole crew is here tonight. The new version of the whole crew. It used to always be me, Dev, Kend, Hallie, and Frannie—Hallie's older sister. But back in February, Frannie met professional football quarterback Mark Abbott on a flight and they had a whirlwind vacation romance without realizing they had ties to the same town upstate, Ida, where Frannie now lives. She still comes down regularly to visit her folks and Hallie—and even more now to be with Mark.

Mark came with two other NFL players, Ryan "Hardy" Hardison and Brian Ackley. Hardy is a wide receiver and Brian is a giant lineman. He looks menacing, but really, he's quiet and kind.

I only met them one other time a couple of months ago when I was here for a job. I only had time to visit for a couple of hours, though. This time, we all have a whole weekend together, and I'm hoping it'll be like the old days. Lots of laughter and shenanigans.

I've missed that.

I don't regret my decision to move home to Georgia a few years ago. The city life isn't for me. Unfortunately, going back home only reminded me why I left. Not all small towns are full of bigotry and hatred, but mine has way too much of that. Since I travel a lot, I've been letting it slide, but as I've been taking on more narration jobs and traveling less, I find myself looking for somewhere else that feels like home.

"What book got all in your head?" Hardy asks. He's a *Bridgerton* nerd and loves all things romance and drama.

"Not a book. A whole ass series."

"Ooh, which one?" Frannie asks, pulling out her phone.

Mark laughs and wraps his arm around her.

"The Mariano Family series by Jade Jackson. Just be aware, it's a rabbit hole, and once you start down it, there's no going back. I started one of her other series on the plane."

"Still got you by the balls?" Devon asks with a laugh.

I shove my shoulder into his. "Fuck off."

"This sounds amazing," Hallie says.

"I was thinking of starting it too," Kennedy says. "Oh. We should start our own book club!"

"Yes!" Frannie throws her hand up. "Baker Girls Book Club."

"Uh, rude. What about the rest of us?" I ask.

Kennedy waves a hand. "Please. You must know by now that you're an honorary Baker girl."

"Thanks?"

All three girls pin me with the same exact glare. They're more like sisters than cousins, especially since their moms are sisters and their dads are brothers.

"Uh, you should be thanking her. It's an honor to be as awesome as us," Hallie sasses.

"Do I get to be an honorary Baker girl too? I want to be in the club!" Hardy says as Brian laughs.

"Of course. We're keeping you forever now," Frannie says.

"Sweet." Hardy smiles as he pulls his black braids into a ponytail, then digs out his phone.

"So, the seventh book isn't the last?" Frannie asks, eyes narrowed on her phone.

"Nope. She's just finishing the eighth."

"He complained about the cliffhanger all morning," Kennedy says.

That was not a cliffhanger. It picked me up, threw me over the cliff, and laughed as I tried to find some rocks to grab on to.

"You don't understand," I groan into my beer bottle.

Hardy plugs his ears. "La la la. Can't hear you. Don't spoil the heartbreak for me."

"This is gonna be fun," Hallie says.

"Can't wait to tell her I've got more souls for her to feed on."

"Wait, did you actually reach out to her?" Kennedy asks.

"Yeah. Slid into her DMs."

"Nice," Hardy says with a grin.

"Not like that."

Okay, a little like that.

I'm not trying to hook up with her, but she's gorgeous, brilliant, and fun to talk to. I'm enjoying myself.

"Aw, Justin has a crush," Hallie sings.

"I—barely know her."

Beside me, Devon snickers.

"I'm telling you, the love bug is coming to bite us all," Frannie says. "Got me. Got Kend and Dev. Maybe it's Justin's turn."

"As long as it's not *my* turn," Hallie says. "I'm happy to watch all you get dopey for love, but not me."

Kennedy and Frannie exchange a look, but it's Hardy who pats her hand and says, "Whatever you say, baby girl."

Hallie vehemently shakes her head. "It makes sense for it to be Mr. Romance over here." She gestures at me. Then she looks past Hardy at Brian. "Or Brian."

Brian looks down at his beer bottle. "You're acting like I'm desperate for love."

Hardy puts his hand on Brian's arm. "Not desperate. But I know you want that, and you deserve to have it."

Brian's head snaps up, and his eyes lock with Hardy's.

Whoa.

Maybe it's my romance brain, but it seems like there's some kind of vibe between the two of them. I assumed they were both straight—which was probably dumb of me—but now I'm wondering if there's something going on there.

But the moment quickly passes, and Kennedy changes the subject.

"So, Hal, how's the nannying going?"

Hallie groans.

"I haven't found another full-time client yet, but between subpoenas and trying to make sure the little girls I used to nanny for have everything they need, I wouldn't have time anyway."

Hallie works as a nanny, but unfortunately, her last job went up in flames when the father cheated on the mother with their overnight nanny. That's led to a bitter divorce, which Hallie, as a former daily member of the household and caregiver to their two young children, has been pulled into the middle of.

"I'll ask around with the team. See if anyone needs anything. Even if it's not full-time, it'll still help you out," Mark says, pulling out his phone.

It's funny, if we'd known them sooner, I can see the football boys being a part of our gang all along, they fit in seamlessly.

My eyes drift back to Hardy and Brian, who are acting normal, but I swear there was a vibe. Maybe I should ask Jade. But when I go to my messages, I find a response from her to a bunch that I sent her earlier.

> I stood in the middle of the airport to finish the last chapter and almost threw my e-reader. I hate you.

> Okay, I've cooled down. I don't hate you. But you're really good at what you do.

JADE JACKSON

I'm glad you enjoyed (?) it.

Laughing to myself, I type out a reply.

> I'm a third of the way through the second book.

JADE JACKSON

I've got you in my clutches now. Have you joined my reader group yet? You can commiserate in there. I think some of my fans have a love-hate relationship with me. I'm not sure why.

> No clue...

> Guess what... I've got some new souls for you to torture.

JADE JACKSON

Oh really?

Yep. My best friend Kennedy, her cousins, and another friend of ours. They're hyped.

JADE JACKSON

Thanks. I appreciate the support.

Full disclosure, it's part support and part needing others to suffer with me.

JADE JACKSON

Fair.

Speaking of which, you get any random sparks of inspiration to finish book eight?

JADE JACKSON

Lol. Not yet.

I suppose demanding you to work all night would be unfair labor practices.

JADE JACKSON

Just a smidge, but my boss has been known to demand those in the past. It's me. I'm the boss.

Sort of speaking of that. I need your romance expertise.

JADE JACKSON

… about what?

I stare at the message for a second then realize how mine sounded. Like I need romance advice for a girl. A girl who isn't her. Which would be shitty. And something I'd never do. Especially because Hallie might not be totally wrong about the crush thing. But I think I should wait and see what happens to decide that.

> Sorry. That sounded scummy. I don't need romance advice, but more your romance eye to see if I'm imagining what I think I'm seeing between two of my friends.

JADE JACKSON

Ooh. Then hit me.

> So they're newer friends and I don't have a lot of context, but it's two guys (neither are out as far as I know), and they're friends. One touched the other's arm and said something nice, then they locked eyes, and for a half a second, I was waiting for them to kiss.

JADE JACKSON

Ooh. Tension. I like it. Um, without knowing them it's hard to say, but it's possible. I'm good at getting a read on people, so feel free to keep telling me if you notice anything else. I'm invested now.

> Good. Something to keep you on the hook. Since we all know you've got me on yours.

JADE JACKSON

JADE JACKSON

You act like it's a bad place to be.

I bite my lip as I read that.

Bite my lip?

Christ, maybe waiting to see if I have a crush is long gone. I think I'm into this girl. Twenty-four hours of talking to her, and I already know I don't want to stop any time soon.

I almost want to ask if she's from New York since it's where her books are set. But I would think asking to meet up while I'm in New York might be a little much.

Then again...

Hey, are you going to be at that signing in Vegas in a couple of weeks?

JADE JACKSON

Yes. Are you?

Yep. Any chance you'd be willing to meet up in person? Also, do you have a pre-order form? I might need to order signed copies of all your books.

JADE JACKSON

I might be open to it. I mean, I won't stop you from coming up to my table, but if you actually want to sit down and hang out... that'd be cool. In a public place.

Of course. I... didn't pause to think about how that might sound. I'm sorry.

JADE JACKSON

No. It's fine. We just don't really know each other well yet. You could be a stalker or a serial killer.

Saying I'm not probably won't prove that, but I'll do my best to prove I don't have any psychopathic tendencies (unlike you). Maybe sprinkle in some details about my life instead of just ranting and raving about your books.

JADE JACKSON

As much as my ego enjoys those things... I wouldn't mind that.

"Whatcha doing?"

I jump as Devon puts his chin on my shoulder, trying to see my phone. I quickly turn the screen off, but when I look up, everyone's eyes are on me.

How long was I messaging Jade?

"Honestly, it's been *months* since you've been here, and now you're ignoring us? Rude," Hallie says, eyes dancing with trouble.

I clear my throat. "Sorry."

"Since we're all here, who is it that you're messaging nonstop?" Dev prods.

I put on my most charming smile. "Just trying to get some spoilers about book eight. Have to have something to hold over your heads."

I turn my phone screen back on and quickly type another text to Jade.

> Sorry. Gotta go. I'm being heckled by my friends.

JADE JACKSON

> All good. My hands are tired. Have fun!

> Night.

"Were you seriously messaging her?" Kennedy asks, eyes alight.

"Who else would it be? All the important people are here," Hallie says.

"Hey, I have a family."

I don't talk to most of them, but still.

"Most of whom you don't like," Devon says. "Speaking of, how's Georgia been?"

I shrug. "Still doesn't feel like home. I don't know why I remembered it being so idyllic. Maybe that's just what I wanted it to be."

"I understand," Kennedy says. "Sometimes you build something up differently in your mind." She flashes a smile at Devon. "Then find out home isn't where or what you thought it was."

Hallie quirks a brow. "I think you had unrealistic expectations and wanted your hometown to be Stars Hollow. Also known as fictional."

"Hey, I think Ida gives some strong Stars Hollow vibes," Frannie says, referencing the little town upstate she moved to a few years ago.

"Agreed. Always loved visiting there as a kid, and getting to live there now, I love it even more," Mark adds.

I chew on my lip, then take a swig of my beer. Would moving to a town I've never been to be crazy?

Maybe.

But I always liked New York, generally speaking. I like the northeast, I love snow, and the summer weather here is less suffocating than down south.

"You know, if you were interested in checking it out or... moving, I happen to know of a couple available apartments," Frannie says. "And the landlord is great."

She looks up at Mark, who smiles at her, then looks at me.

"Yeah, I bought Frannie's building a couple of months ago. We renovated the top floor into a penthouse, so her apartment and the one across from it will both be available at the beginning of July. One is yours if you want it."

I spin my beer bottle, thinking it through. My mom will complain endlessly, but what else is new?

"You know, I think I might take you up on that."

Kennedy laughs. "Frannie's just trying to move the whole friend group there."

"Hey, I know you're happy in Brighton. Maybe I'll convince you to retire in Ida, though." She winks at her cousin, then looks to me. "No pressure. But keep it in mind if you need a change of pace."

Should I do it?

What is there for me in Georgia?

Not much. Not the home I've been craving.

"Two bedrooms?" I ask.

Frannie nods. "Yep."

"Can I turn one into a recording studio?"

Mark shrugs. "Fine by me."

I take another swig of my beer.

Fuck it.

"Sign me up."

Frannie claps her hands. "I'm so excited! You really will love it. No rush to move in, just let us know when you're ready."

"I'll start packing as soon as I'm home and plan for the move after I get back from Las Vegas."

"Sounds good. We'll have it ready for you," Mark says.

I give him a nod in thanks.

It's crazy, but life's too short not to take risks. Even if I don't love it, I doubt it'll be any worse than where I am now. And at least I'll have a friend nearby.

Who knows, maybe I'll get lucky and live out my own small-town romance.

But when I think that, my eyes drift down to my phone, and I think of Jade. Of the picture of her looking gorgeous surrounded by books. It would be delusional to believe that there'll be anything between us. But if life as a romance lover has taught me anything, it's that you can't predict how and when love will find you, and you can't stop the free fall into its hold once it does.

CHAPTER FIVE

Jade

THREE CUTE DRESSES. Check.

One fancier dress. Check.

I really only need a dress for the signing and a dress for the mixer the night before, since I travel looking dumpster-chic at best, but I like to have options. Plus... I want to have something cute to meet Justin in. Even if it's just two online friends meeting up, I can still look cute.

Speaking of Justin, my phone dings again.

We've moved past messaging on social media, and we exchanged phone numbers a couple of days ago. Now we text.

JUSTIN

Question... do you have anyone assisting you at the signing? I'm signing at the narrator event in the morning, but I'm free for the rest of the day. If you're comfortable with it, and don't have anyone to help, I'd be happy to step in. Plus, you know I can fangirl about your books. Unless you're tired of listening to me do that.

I'm never tired of hearing you talk about my books. That's always fun for me. Especially when I tease you with what might come next.

JUSTIN

So you're saying you like edging me?

I blink at my phone several times. Talking with him tends to have a flirtatious side, but that's a little more overt than we've been. Not that I necessarily mind.

Unfortunately, though, that's mostly because my parasocial crush morphed into a real crush, and it grows the more I talk to Justin. Especially as we sprinkle more details about ourselves in. He seems like a good guy.

Obviously, I'm not going to believe that until I meet him in person and check the vibes. Men are excellent pretenders, and there can be predatory ones in the romance community. I refuse to fall victim to that.

JUSTIN

Sorry. That was too far.

Again, I stare at my phone, unsure how to respond. I don't mind having fun. But boundaries are still necessary until we know each other better.

No worries. I walked right into it.

Plus, edging is part of my job as an author.

To keep from going anywhere more than that playful space, I quickly change topic.

> But back to your question, no, I don't have anyone assisting me. I'm coming with my friends, Zoey and Trish. Zoey is also an author and Trish is her lifelong bestie. Trish does some social media stuff for me and offered to help assist me at the event, but I think she'll primarily be with Zoey. Short answer is: sure. Assuming you pass my vibe check.

JUSTIN

> More than fair. You'll be there tomorrow, right? Want to meet up tomorrow night? Assess the vibes?

> LOL. Sure. Just let me know what time.

JUSTIN

> Sounds good. We can meet at the hotel bar. Should be nice and public. Feel free to bring your friends if it makes you more comfortable.

> Thanks.

I get back to packing, making sure I have plenty of shoe options available. After checking those off, I head for the bathroom and pack up all my cosmetics. I'm a makeup girl through and through. It started as a way to boost my self-confidence when I was young. Then an act of rebellion against my mom who hates makeup. Now it's a part of me. I'm fine if I don't wear it, but it's a fun part of my routine, and I love how I get to play with colors and styles of makeup, give off an entirely different persona depending on the choices I make. Usually I keep it simple, but it's always fun to explore and experiment.

From the other room, my phone pings, and when I get back, I laugh out loud at the message Justin sent.

JUSTIN

Okay, I know this is random, but… have you ever thought of having Evvie, Taylor, and Josh end up in a polyamorous relationship?

It takes me a second to stop laughing about that. It's cute how invested in my characters he is. He'll be excited to know that the back half of book eight leads into Evvie's story. She's a character I've been dying to write more of ever since the end of the second book when her husband Josh cheated on her with her best friend Taylor. Since then, her story has mostly been about healing herself and living her life. She hasn't been a central focus for a couple of books, but there's still plenty of tension there, and with her coming back to town after a healing journey, I'm excited to dive back in.

The thought of typing out all my thoughts in response to that is too much, so I click on the voice note and continue packing as I answer him.

"Actually, yes. But it didn't occur to me until book three, and as much as I love the idea, I didn't lay any groundwork for a relationship between Taylor and Evvie. And that's the only way I could do it. Tay and Josh would have to realize how much they love her and fight for her. Because otherwise, it would just be Josh getting the best of both worlds and Evvie going back to him after he cheated on her. Not something I can get behind. And I don't think I could randomly add the right amount of tension in there now. It wouldn't be believable. Buttttt I also have the most perfect ending for Evvie, so stay tuned. But back to the poly thing, I keep thinking I want to do some sort of One Tree Hill retelling where Brooke, Lucas, and Peyton are in a poly relationship."

The three little dots appear, and after a moment, another message comes through.

JUSTIN

I would read the fuck out of that.

The idea has been dancing around in my brain forever. I look down at my aching hand. If only I had more time. Though I will need something new for my subscription service at the beginning of next year.

> Hmm. Maybe it's something I should do for my subscription service.

JUSTIN

> Hold up. How did I not know you have one of those? Literally running to sign up.

He adds a little running man emoji to the end of his text. I appreciate the support, even if it feels a little strange as I become friends with someone.

Taking strangers' money is fine. Taking your friends' money will always feel weird. It's why Zo and I trade books. We both feel icky asking the other to pay.

"Jade? You here?" my dad calls from the living room.

"Yeah. Be out in a sec."

I check off the couple of items I just packed, then set my list back on the bed. Grabbing my phone, I aim for the living room.

"Hey, Dad. What's up?" I give him a quick hug and follow him to the kitchen.

"Thought I'd bring you a little something for dinner tonight and breakfast tomorrow so you don't have to worry about ordering out. Pre-made breakfast sandwich and hash browns for the morning. Just microwave and go. And some lasagna for dinner tonight."

"You're the best. Thank you. Mm. Feel free to put a whole pan of lasagna in my freezer."

He laughs. "Maybe you'll come back to a surprise or two."

I laugh too, but my attention shifts to my phone as it goes off.

JUSTIN

BTW please tell me if I'm ever annoying you
with all my random thoughts and feelings
about your characters.

Feel free to keep messaging me random
thoughts. It makes me smile.

I don't know if I should say that or not, but we're talking about more than books these days, and... it's the truth.

JUSTIN

If it makes you smile, I'll message you my
random thoughts all day.

Damn. I guess I should expect the swoony stuff from a guy who loves reading romance as much as I do, but still. It makes me feel all melty inside.

It's not until after I've made some kind of happy little squeak that I remember I'm not alone in my kitchen.

I look up to find my dad's eyes fixed on me.

"Who are you talking to?"

I clear my throat and set my phone down. "Just a friend."

"A friend, huh? Is this friend a boy?"

"Dad. I'm not fifteen."

"So, that's a yes. Do I get to meet him?"

"I haven't even met him yet."

Dad's brows lift, and I slap a hand over my mouth. *Whoops.*

Then Dad's grinning at me, and I don't have to ask where I get my troublemaking smile from.

"But you're planning on meeting him?"

"We're. Just. Friends. But yes. He'll be at the convention this weekend. He's a narrator. And cover model," I mutter.

"Well, as long as he treats you right, I approve of your *friendship.*"

"Dad, I'm thirty years old."

"And no matter how old you are, I'll always want the best for you." He kisses the side of my head. "By the way, I brought your mail up. I think I saw something from your insurance company in there."

I scramble for the pile of mail and find the letter with my insurance company's logo on it. They've been giving me a ton of crap about my surgery for the past two weeks. They instantly denied paying for it, so I had to send in more information. Then that still wasn't enough, and I had to send in a second appeal with more information.

The woman on the phone last time assured me they had everything they need, so it should be...

Denied?

My heart slams against my ribs. They're denying it?

Oh, no. They're not just denying my surgery, they're denying any related follow-ups with my doctor, and any physical or occupational therapy related.

Then there's the damning bolded two words. *Final decision.*

Tears rush to my eyes.

When my dad turns from the refrigerator and sees me, he crosses the room to me. "What is it?"

"They denied the surgery."

"What?" he demands, taking the letter as I pull out my phone and, with shaking hands, dial the number for my insurance company's help line.

Of course, I'm put on hold. Usually it's anywhere between twenty and forty minutes before I get through to someone.

When my dad finishes reading the letter, he hands it back to me. I pace the apartment, reading the letter over and over while I'm on hold. Dad tries to busy himself unloading and loading the dishwasher, but I can feel his eyes on me.

There's all kinds of stupid medical and legal jargon that don't make any sense to me.

I pay this company thousands of dollars a year, and they aren't covering this?

No. This has to be wrong. I need this surgery. Do they think I just want to do it for fun? Because not being able to use my dominant hand for over a month doesn't sound fun to me.

When the line finally connects, I force myself to be calm, willing my voice not to shake, and reminding myself not to yell at the person on the phone because it's not their fault.

The woman is deeply apologetic as she does her best to explain the letter. It's clear she disagrees with their decision. She tells me seeing another specialist, going through what I've already done to try to prevent surgery again, and then scheduling a surgery with a different doctor is my only hope, but even then, it's unlikely. And it would take too long. Who knows how much more I would suffer in that time.

A mix of fury and sadness wars within me as I hang up the phone. Grabbing my laptop, I sit down on my couch and do some rage researching.

Six to eight *thousand* dollars. That's how much the surgery will cost out of pocket, and that doesn't include any extra little things they might try to charge me for. It doesn't include any of my follow-ups or therapy which will be thousands of dollars more.

I jump over to my bank account and look through all my finances. The monthly income I give myself won't cover that. Not by a longshot. Then I look at the one account I don't want to touch. The one for my audiobook savings. This would be anywhere from a quarter to a third of that. Assuming everything goes okay.

"Honey," Dad whispers, sitting down next to me as I sniffle. "It'll be okay. We'll figure it out. We could do one of those online fundraiser things."

I slowly shake my head at that. "We don't have that much reach that it'll make a difference. And I am not asking my readers for this. There's something inherently wrong about that to me. It's not like I'm dying. I'll just have to figure it out."

Audiobooks will have to wait.

That guts me, but it is what it is.

If I can't type without horrible pain, I can't keep doing this anyway. There's no other choice, no matter what my insurance company thinks.

Now I have to hope that this doesn't completely derail my career and force me to burn through even more of the money I've been saving up.

CHAPTER SIX

Jade

A NICE SHOWER, curling my hair, and doing my makeup fixes almost any problem I have.

Maybe not *fixes*, but it wraps a bandage around the wound.

When I get dolled up and dressed up, I end up feeling better. Dress for the attitude I want, not the attitude I have. It's silly, but it's always worked for me.

I remember the first time I told Zoey that. She thought I was crazy. But she rarely wears makeup and is one of those people who can wake up with her hair looking perfect. She's also a mom of two boys who run her ragged, so comfort makes her feel best.

I love that for her, and I love that it makes her feel sexy and confident.

That's the same vibe I need tonight. It's about feeling cute and flirty and having fun to take my mind off all the other bullshit in life.

Zoey, Trish, and I landed in Las Vegas almost two hours ago, and in a few minutes, I'm going to meet Justin. I haven't mentioned that to them yet. I'm a little worried I'm making it more of a thing than it needs to be. For all I know, he'll show up in exercise shorts and an undershirt and be a total tool.

Somehow I doubt it, though.

I went radio silent after getting that letter from my insurance company. I put do not disturb mode on and ignored the world for a while because I can't process shit when I feel like there's something I'm supposed to be doing, or someone I'm supposed to be talking to. Instead, after my dad left, I finished packing, dug a piece of frozen raspberry chocolate tart from my freezer, warmed it up, and enjoyed every sinful bite, then I went to my room, got out a couple of my favorite toys and had two killer orgasms. It's hard to be upset about anything when you're too blissed out to move.

When I finally remembered to turn do not disturb mode off late last night, I had a bunch of texts from Justin checking in. I didn't say much back, and he continued to check in today. None of it felt pushy, but rather like genuine concern. I reassured him I was okay, and I was looking forward to meeting up with him tonight.

Which I am.

I think he'll pass the vibe check, but I'm not sure what to expect from this. A friendly hang out? A cute dinner date? A hookup?

Would I hook up with him?

Yes. In a heartbeat. If he's who he seems to be, he's gorgeous, sweet, and respectful. Three out of three ain't bad.

Plus, imagining his sinful drawl in the bedroom...

Okay, I need to stop.

We're friends. Friendly-ish friend-like people.

That's all.

But damn if I don't look sexy as fuck anyway.

I knock on the door that adjoins my room and Zoey and Trish's. Once we all tried staying in the same room, but we were on top of each other. Waiting for the shower took forever, and planning our schedule around that was a pain in the ass.

Plus, I like my alone time.

Orgasms. I like orgasms.

I rarely go a day without getting off and frequently do it more than once a day. I almost always bring toys with me when I travel, and this trip is no different. Sharing a room with your friends when you're horny as fuck is not fun.

Trish whistles as she opens the door.

"You look gorgeous."

I shrug. It's a simple dress and wedges. Nothing fancy. My makeup is low-key, except around my eyes where I have a pretty pink and orange eye shadow blend that matches my dress.

"This isn't much."

Zoey looks over as I walk into the room. "I beg to disagree. But it's not a surprise. You always look gorgeous. Headed somewhere?"

I clear my throat. "Uh, yeah. I'm meeting Justin down at the bar."

"Justin Ayers?" Trish squeaks.

"Yes," I say flatly.

"I love this for you." She claps her hands.

From behind her, Zoey laughs.

"Is it friends or more?"

"Friends," I say quickly. Probably too quickly.

"Mhm. I'll believe that if you're in your room tomorrow morning when I wake up." Trish winks at me. She's an early riser and usually wakes Zoey and me up for early breakfast and work-outs on our trips.

"I'll be there." My voice is firm, but the truth is, if Justin wanted me in his room tonight, that's where I'd be.

And now I'm horny. A little bit.

This train of thought needs to stop right now.

"We'll see," Trish says.

Zoey shakes her head. "Have fun. Be safe. You'll just be at the hotel bar?"

"To start. If we grab food or something, I'll text you."

She nods. Zoey never exits mom mode, but I appreciate that she's always looking out for us.

"She's right. Be safe. We love you. Have fun. Be good."

As I walk through the door back into my room, Trish calls one last thing.

"Or be bad."

I shake my head as the door clicks, but I can't deny being bad sounds fun.

I'M CHRONICALLY EARLY.

I was late to middle school once, and my principal was on a warpath after being continuously disrespected by a bunch of students, so I ended up with a week full of lunch detention because it was unexcused. As the good girl who always followed the rules, I was miserable.

So, I made it a point to never be late again. Now it's a problem because I'm often fifteen minutes early.

I'm only eight minutes early to the bar. That's reasonable, at least.

"What can I get you?" a bartender asks as I lean against the counter.

I'm not risking sitting on one of the sleek but not particularly sturdy looking stools.

I hate furniture that looks nice but is impractical and barely holds any weight. I also hate that those thoughts ever run through my mind, but unfortunately, the world isn't built for plus-size people. Just like how I have to go out of my way when I need a belt extender on an airplane. It should be able to be requested in advance and waiting at your seat. But that's life being a fat person in a thin person's world.

I glance up at the menu. They have a bunch of fun specials that are meant to be romance-themed, though I wish they'd come up with cutesy names too. It would make them stand out more.

"I'll have a frozen pomegranate margarita."

"Coming right up."

The bartender goes to make my drink, and I instantly feel a presence at my side.

I don't know how, but I can tell it's not Justin. Maybe because the energy feels too... smarmy.

"Pomegranate margarita, huh?"

I turn my head ever so slightly and see a tallish decently attractive guy. He's staring at me with a look that makes my stomach turn.

This is why I rarely go to bars. I'd rather make drinks at home with my friends. Thank God there're apps for hooking up now, so I don't have to worry about going to bars for that.

"Yep."

Ah, the dilemma of how to engage with a guy who clearly thinks I owe him something. Ignoring him or pissing him off can both be dangerous, but anything else can be too inviting. Thankfully, the bar isn't too busy yet, so I can get the bartender's full attention if I need it.

"Pomegranate. The fruit of sexual awakening."

Oh god.

"I hadn't heard that before," I say coolly.

I *have.* But I haven't heard someone say it in such an icky way.

Smarmy. My first impression was dead on.

"You must not be here for the romance convention, then."

"I take it you are?" I still don't look at him, and I keep my voice bored. There's no way I'm telling this guy I'm an author.

"I am. I'm the romance guy. Darren Corval. I put the *man* in romance."

I fight to keep my face neutral. Could he sound like more of a dick? I recognize the name, though. He's an influencer who made a name for himself as a male "romance-lover." I know plenty of people who love his content and know a few authors who have worked with him. Something about him always made me feel icky, though. Clearly, that was dead-on.

"Here you are." The bartender sets my drink in front of me and meets my gaze. "Need anything else?"

"I'm okay right now. I'll let you know if I do."

He glances behind me, then gives me a curt nod and walks to the other end of the bar to wait on someone.

Ignoring the creep at my side, I take a sip of my drink.

"Taste good?"

I jump as his voice tickles my ear and his hand lands on my ass.

Then a booming voice rings out from my other side.

"What the fuck do you think you're doing?"

CHAPTER SEVEN

Justin

THE GROWL that rips from my throat sends the shitstain of a human with his hand on Jade's ass skittering backward.

Darren Corval. He's a sniveling fuckwad. I've heard stories about him from authors, including one I've worked with a lot who'd worked with him as an "influencer" to help promote one of her books. She refuses to work with him now. No fucking wonder.

Jade swings from staring at me wide-eyed to glaring at the prick.

As much as I want to pull her protectively into my arms, I need to deal with this scummy sack of shit first.

I stalk over to him, getting right in his face.

"Why the fuck do you think you have a right to touch any woman without their consent?"

He sneers at me. "How do you know I didn't have her consent?"

"Because I watched her jump when you touched her."

"You want me to have him thrown out?" the bartender asks.

"Not unless you can get him thrown out of the romance convention too," I grit out.

"Already working on that." Jade's voice is calm and in control as she taps away on her phone. "I'm talking to the organizers right now."

Fuck yes, she is.

"Go to your room. Pack your shit. Leave. If I see you hanging around the romance con, I'll be sure this hotel throws you out, and you're blacklisted from every reader event possible."

"Fuck you," he spits at me. Then as he walks by Jade, he mutters, "Like I'd want anything to do with her disgusting fat ass anyway."

"What did you—"

Jade steps in front of me and puts a hand on my chest. "Let him go."

"But he—"

"I know. He's a piece of shit. But you punching him will only help him look like a victim. Let him go. The organizers will handle it from here."

My eyes drift down and skate over her gorgeous face, and finally, my body relaxes.

God, she's stunning.

"Hi," she whispers.

I let out a heavy laugh. "Hi. Not the way I wanted our first meeting to go."

She smiles at me. "Me either. But you've officially passed my vibe check. Thank you. I could've handled it, but men standing up to other men who pull that shit matters. When men say it's not okay and ostracize other men for doing it, that makes a difference."

I look at her sincerely. "No one should ever have to feel uncomfortable getting a drink or doing anything else. And especially here at a romance con—"

"I know. This is a safe space, and he's a predator in it. Even if it doesn't happen today, eventually karma will get him." She breathes out and shakes her body like she's shaking it all off. Then she looks over at the bar. "Can I get another drink? That one feels tainted now."

The bartender gives an understanding nod. "No problem."

"Put it on my room tab. 428. And I'll have a... watermelon mojito."

The bartender nods. "If you want to have a seat, someone will bring those over."

"Does that extend to outside too?" Jade asks, eyeing the doors out onto the stone terrace.

"Sure thing."

"Thanks," she says.

I offer her my arm. "Shall we?"

She laughs a little. "Yes."

"ANYWAY, that's how I got started publishing. I might never have done it without that support from my dad."

"I'll have to remember to thank Papa Jackson if I ever get to meet him. It would be a crime for your books not to have made it into the world."

Her cheeks heat, like they have every single time I've given her a compliment tonight. It's clear she's not great at taking them, which is all the more reason I'm going to shower her with them. She deserves to hear them and believe them so she knows how amazing she is. Even more so in person. And her voice... I've been fixated on how beautiful it is since that one little voice note she sent me. Now that we're here together, I could listen to her talk all night.

"I'm sure he'll love the nickname."

"I'm assuming you two are close, then?"

"Definitely. We've been each other's rocks for a long time. It's always a safe space with us. I'm lucky to have that. What about you? Close with your parents?"

She shifts in the chair and tucks her legs up, making sure her dress covers everything. I've lost track of how long we've been sitting here. We've had drinks, appetizers, and dinner, talking the whole time. Everything I enjoyed about talking with Jade over the past couple of weeks is amplified now in her company.

I drag my teeth over my bottom lip and shake my head. "No. We have very different views on life, and having a close relationship with them would be impossible without a lot of toxicity, so I keep things more at arm's length."

Mom's been plenty pissed at me since I told her I was moving. But other than a dinner at their house that I suffered through every couple of weeks, we don't have any connection tying us together.

"I'm sorry to hear that," Jade says, her voice gentle and sincere.

I shrug. "I'm used to it. I compartmentalized a lot of my parents' behavior. It wasn't until I moved home that I noticed it. Which is probably why I'm moving again. Speaking of which, I've been meaning to ask you, do you live in New York? I assumed so since most of your stories are set there."

"Yeah. A tiny little two-stoplight town called Woods Junction. Most of my stories are based on surrounding towns, but my very first series of interconnected standalones are set in a town just like it."

"But not the Marianos?" I ask.

She laughs. "Nope."

"You know... if you need any beta readers for book eight, I volunteer as tribute. I'll sign an NDA. Whatever you want."

She stares at me for a long moment. "I might take you up on that." Then she sighs. "It really depends if you're comfortable reading it without knowing when you'll get book nine."

My brow furrows at the hitch in her voice. She doesn't work with a publisher as far as I know, so there shouldn't be anyone stepping in to say she can't release something.

"Writer's block?"

I don't know what else it could be.

She looks to the side at a fountain in the courtyard. "No. Believe me, I know what I want to write and it's killing me that I'll have to wait, but I have a severe case of carpal tunnel. I have to have surgery for it in a little over a week, and I'll be out of typing commission for three to four weeks, and it'll be even longer before I can type as much as I used to."

Shit.

"I'm sorry. That must be hard."

She nods. "I have so many ideas in my head, and having to get through with voice notes when all I want to do is write—have the catharsis I need—kills me. And I suck at dictation. So here I am. I was hoping to at least get the process of audiobooks for the Mariano Family series started during that time, but now that won't be happening either."

"Why not?"

She laughs bitterly. "I was saving up so I could have all eight done, and then save up the rest for the last few books while those are being produced. But my insurance company decided that covering my surgery and all the therapy I'll need after isn't something they're interested in, so I'll have to dig into the money I was saving for audiobooks to do that."

"What the fuck?"

Her eyes go wide, then she smiles softly. "It is what it is."

"It's not. It's bullshit. Where is your insurance through?"

"I'm self-employed. So I self-pay. I'll be looking at new options when my enrollment is up in January, but until then, I'm stuck."

Leaning back in my chair, I shake my head. Insurance in this country is beyond fucked up. I'm lucky I get mine through my cousin. She runs a law firm, and since I gave her some money to help found it back when I first started modeling, she keeps me on the books, and I help with their commercials and advertising whether it be modeling or voice over. It's a small chunk of my income, but they have great insurance and that's a huge plus.

Now I'm pissed for Jade, and I wish there was something I could do to help her.

She waves a hand as if she's swatting away a bug.

"Can we change topic? I found out yesterday and spent all night wallowing—that's why I didn't respond much. I want to enjoy this weekend, not think about all that."

"Of course." I glance over at the courtyard, which is lit up with twinkle lights. "Up for a walk?"

She smiles brightly. "Yeah. Sounds great."

I stand and hold out my hand to her. She stands too, and the second her skin brushes against mine, a crack of electricity ripples through me, aiming straight for my heart.

She must feel it too, because she freezes for a second before lacing her fingers with mine.

"How did you get into narrating?" Jade asks as we step off the terrace and onto the path that winds through the courtyard.

"Combination of things. My cousin Stacy had been suggesting it for years. She runs a law firm, and I do the narration for most of their commercials and radio ads. Then as I started getting attention for my book covers, I had some authors tell me my voice would be perfect for their books. I love the romance community, and the idea of narrating sounded fun to me, and like a complement to working as a model. I took some voice acting classes first to make sure I had the skill to back it up, and I also took a course on audiobook production. It was an investment to build out my recording area and to get the production software, but as soon as I started doing it, I fell in love. It's so much fun."

"Zoey tells me I should consider narrating audiobooks—particularly some of my own—but I don't know..."

"You should. You have a beautiful voice."

Again, her cheeks heat. "That's something coming from you."

I chuckle at that. "You like southern drawl, darlin'?"

She tries and fails to hide a shiver. "Maybe. But I've heard books you've narrated without it, and you still have a captivating voice. You're excellent with emotional work too. That's something I look for."

"With your books, you have to. If I ever get a chance, I'd be honored to record one of your books."

"Thanks," she breathes. "What made you pick up the Mariano Family series?"

"Oh, darlin', I am just like every other voracious reader out there. A good hook will get me. I believe it was the one about Lizzie, with her walking into the apartment after her prodigal mother returned, only to find her ex-fiancé Alex standing there... yeah. I had to know all the drama."

"I laughed so hard writing that scene. Lizzie is so done with everything, and she just grabs a bottle of wine, lets her siblings in, and walks away, leaving Alex to the wolves."

"I love their story, though. Earning back trust. Exploring what unconditional love truly means. It was beautifully done."

She lets out a little huff. "I feel like all you've done tonight is compliment me."

"Because you're brilliant, and you should know that."

Leaning in, I press a gentle kiss to her cheek, and her sharp inhale goes straight to my dick.

I need to calm down.

As fun as it would be to take Jade upstairs and keep her in my bed all night, I really like her. I want more than one night, which means taking it slowly.

"Well, if you're still open to assisting me on Saturday, you've officially passed all my vibe checks."

I bite back a smile. "Good to know. And I'd love to help you and convince everyone to buy your books. Need any help setting up tomorrow?"

"That would actually be great. I'm not supposed to lift much."

"How are you going to sign—"

"I have a stamp and already warned my readers that if they didn't pre-order, I would only have stamped books for the signing, nothing personalized. I hate it, but it's the best I can do."

"It's more than enough. Don't beat yourself up about it. You need to take care of yourself, so you can keep writing books for us to love."

She looks up at me for a moment, but doesn't say anything. As we continue on our walk, though, she gives my hand the slightest squeeze, causing heat to burn in my gut all over again.

AFTER WALKING through the courtyard and back through the hotel, we're standing outside Jade's hotel room, tension swamping the air around us.

"I had fun tonight. Thank you for... everything."

"It was my pleasure, darlin'." Her breath hitches at the word, and I tuck that information away. *She likes it.*

My hands are wrapped around hers as she gazes up at me.

"I'm looking forward to tomorrow," I rumble. *Because apparently I rumble things now.*

"Me too."

She stares at me for a beat longer, then her grip on one of my hands tightens as her other hand snakes up my arm and she leans up on her toes, pressing her soft lips into my cheek.

Warmth erupts in my gut, and it takes everything in me not to pin her to the wall and feel her lips against mine, swallow her sinful moans, and let her feel every inch of me.

But we're not there yet. So, I savor every second of her lips touching my skin until she pulls away, landing back on flat feet.

"See you tomorrow."

"Tomorrow."

She locks eyes with me one last time, her hand still wrapped around my arm, then she turns toward the door, her fingers leaving a trail of sparks on my skin as she slowly lets me go and walks inside.

I stare at her closed door for too long before I finally force my feet to move. Elevator. Up two floors. Then I'm back in my room.

I collapse on my bed, completely overwhelmed. Everything I felt about Jade while we were texting was the tip of the iceberg.

I imagined hooking up, maybe even a date. I didn't imagine my heart leaping out of my chest like it was trying to get to hers.

It takes all my effort to undress and get ready for bed, but the second I'm there, my mind is back on Jade. She looked effortlessly beautiful tonight, and the chemistry between us was palpable. I thought I felt sparks when her hand was in mine, but then she kissed my cheek, and I've never known desire like that before.

My cock thickens, and even though I shouldn't, I'm shameless as I slip my hand in my boxers and stroke my length, imagining Jade's silky lips on my cheek, my lips, my chest. Wrapped around my cock.

Just the thought makes me shudder with desperation.

Working myself from base to tip, I swipe my thumb across, smearing the pre-cum. The fantasy is too easy to get lost in. Her soft curves under my hard body. My fingers digging into her full hips as she rides me. The way her shimmering maple eyes would roll back as she came.

"Fuck," I grunt.

I stroke myself harder until my spine tingles and my balls tighten.

My release coats my hand as I come to the thought of Jade naked, covered in my cum. *Mine.*

I am so screwed.

As I come down, my mind clears, and after cleaning up, I'm fixated on what Jade said tonight about her insurance.

A little too wired, I grab my phone and start researching. There has to be another option. She shouldn't have to pay thousands of dollars out of pocket when she has insurance. But the deeper I dig, the less useful information I find.

It's not until I'm settled in bed, almost asleep, that the perfect solution filters into my brain. So perfect I can't believe I didn't think of it before. I'll have to do a little more research tomorrow, but if I'm right, I might've found the solution to Jade's problems.

CHAPTER EIGHT

Jade

YES.

Justin's devastating smirk dances in my mind as I imagine his firm body rolling over mine as he thrusts into me.

I mimic the movements I crave with the silicone cock, hitting the deepest part of my core as my vibrator perfectly teases my clit.

A scream builds in my chest, but I bite my lip, holding it back. These walls are thin, and no one else needs to know that I'm getting myself off to the thought of the sweet, caring, playful Greek god of a man I spent the evening with.

I've never been complimented so much in such a short time. Never had someone look at me the way he did. The way a man should look at a woman. Like she's the only thing worth his time.

Justin made me feel treasured, desired, like there was no woman on the planet as meaningful to him as me.

It's insanity to think that, to believe it. But the look in his eyes after I kissed his cheek? It was the wanton desire I've written so many times, but never gotten to see.

When I kissed his cheek, fire blazed through me, and I wanted so much more.

It was right not to pursue it. We're building a friendship and maybe the potential for something more.

That doesn't mean I can't fantasize though. After how hot I was for him tonight, I have to take the edge off.

Twice.

The first time was fast, just working my vibrator over my clit, but it wasn't enough. I want to live the fucking I didn't get to have vicariously through a blue silicone dildo.

"Fuck," I mutter, stomach clenching as beads of sweat form between my breasts.

My nipples could use some love too, but since my hands are occupied, I'll have to make do.

I swirl my hips as I reposition the vibrator and pull the dildo out before shoving it all the way in again.

Faster. More.

My eyes drift closed as I imagine Justin splayed beneath me as I ride him.

Fuck, I love to ride.

I fight back a whimper, my core tightening as my body lights on fire.

So close. I'm so close and so desperate.

My body shakes as I rock against the vibrator, riding the blue cock until I'm bursting at the seams.

I clamp my mouth shut as I come undone, keeping every moan locked away as my toes curl into the sheets and I arch off the bed.

Slowly, my muscles relax, and I turn the vibrator off, then pull the dildo out and stare at it, slick and sticky.

Maybe one day it'll actually be Justin's cock. If it was, I'd be completely feral and suck every drop off him afterward.

That's almost enough to turn me on again, but I'm wiped. It's been a long day, and I need to sleep so I'll be ready for tomorrow.

After getting cleaned up, I nestle under the covers, sated and happy. And because I'm a hopeless lost cause, I fall asleep dreaming of a love story with Justin.

ZOEY, Trish, and I weave through the tables in the grand ballroom where the signing event is happening tomorrow.

After a fun panel this morning about writing a series—which Zoey and I were on and Trish moderated—it's set up time.

"There she is," Justin croons as I make my way toward the table I'll be at. Zoey and Trish will be at the table next to me.

"Hey." I manage to keep my voice calm, even though I feel all breathy and lightheaded, especially knowing I came thinking about him last night. "This is Trish Davies and Zoey Holloway."

He shakes both of their hands. "Pleasure to meet you, ladies. Zoey, I've read your romantasy series. I really enjoyed it. Looking forward to the next book."

"Thanks," Zoey says. Then her face morphs into a wicked smirk. "Glad you enjoyed it. Just not enough to slide into my DMs."

My eyes flare wide and I elbow her in the side as Trish chokes on a laugh.

Justin chuckles too, then he wraps his arm around me. "What can I say? Jade has a hold on me."

My whole body flushes red at his words.

I wonder if I have the same kind of hold on him he had on me while I came on that blue dildo last night.

"Of course she does. She's awesome," Trish says. "Take care of our girl."

"No problem. Come on, darlin'." Justin walks to the other end of my table and opens one of the totes.

Darlin', Trish mouths excitedly.

"This is going to be fun to watch play out," Zoey says.

"I hate you both," I sing.

"No, you don't. You love us." Trish waves her hands to shoo me away. "Go have some fun."

I shake my head, but follow Justin to the other end of the table.

"Where should I start?" he asks.

"Table runner, then you can put the lighter boxes with stickers and signs on the table and I'll set those up." I pull my phone out. "And here's a picture from my last signing for how I set up my books."

"Got it."

Everything comes together fairly quickly, and though we don't talk much, every so often one of us catches the other staring.

As we finish up, we both reach for the last book, and our fingers brush. My gaze snaps to his, and I swear I can see the sparks dancing in the air around us. The tension between us is palpable.

Pulling the book toward me, I place it in its spot, trying to shake off the overheated, lightheaded feeling that swamps me after a tiny touch from Justin.

"I think that's everything." I stand back and look at the table.

"Want to grab some lunch?" Trish asks, walking over with Zoey.

"Sure. But can we be totally cheesy and stop by the book arch to take pictures first? It'll be too crazy tomorrow."

"Oh yeah. We have to," Zoey says. "I love the book arch. It's the perfect blend of whimsical and timeless."

"You should have one at your wedding," I say dreamily to Trish.

She thinks for a second. "Maybe if it wasn't going to be

outside at Mama and Papa O's. I don't know how well it would hold up outdoors. Plus, what if it rains?" Trish elbows Zoey. "Maybe you should have one at *your* wedding."

"Are you engaged too?" Justin asks.

Zoey sighs heavily. "No. She just likes to cause trouble."

Justin's eyes move between the three of us. "No wonder the three of you are such good friends."

I put a hand to my chest in mock offense. "Excuse me. I'm not a troublemaker. I'm a good girl."

Justin bites his lip, then leans down and whispers, "I'll bet you are."

Oh, shit.

I cause trouble. I'm in trouble. So much trouble everywhere.

When we get out to the book arch, we take turns snapping individual and group photos. After I take one of Justin with Zoey and Trish, I hand him back his phone, but he gives me that devilish smile that melts me.

"Don't I get one with you?"

"Of course," I squeak. Then I clear my throat. "Let's do it."

We walk over to the book arch and settle in the middle of it. Justin wraps his hand around my waist, but when his fingers dig into my side and he inches me closer, my breath catches.

That's not how he stood with Trish and Zoey.

He did the Keanu Reeves thing where he put his hands out flat with his arms behind them, but obviously not touching them.

But me? He's touching me.

And every glorious inch of his body touching mine has me on fire.

This is beyond being in trouble. With every second I spend with him, I want more. When he touches me, I want to rip my clothes off and explore the depth of the connection between us.

I'm emotionally charged, wildly uninhibited, and absolutely intoxicated with him.

That's a dangerous place to be.

LUNCH WAS... tense.

We laughed. We had a good time. But every time Zoey and Trish weren't looking, Justin's eyes were on me. Or mine were on him. Or both.

Then he gently grazed his hand over my thigh when he asked if he could pay.

That same hand has been on my lower back the entire walk—and elevator ride—back to my room.

It's fine.

It's not like I'm going to spontaneously combust or anything.

"Thanks for lunch," Zoey says, as we get to our rooms.

"No problem. I appreciate y'all keeping me company. Despite being in this world for a while, I don't actually have too many author friends, and only a couple of narrator ones."

"We're happy to claim you," Trish says. Then her eyes meet mine. "Jade, did you want to come over and watch a movie before the mixer tonight?"

Justin's hand slides off my back, and he angles his body so he can meet my eyes. "Actually, if you have a few minutes, I wanted to talk to you about something. Here or in my room. Whatever works."

The heat of Zoey's and Trish's stares burn into me, but I ignore them.

"Sure. We can go to your room."

I'm not trying to be forward, but the walls are thin, and unless we're whispering, Zoey and Trish will be able to hear everything. Not that I'm expecting to rip our clothes off and jump into bed, but whatever this conversation is, should be private.

He holds out his arm. "Right this way then, darlin'."

Zoey flares her eyes at me as Trish pumps her eyebrows.

"I'll text you later," I call as Justin leads me away.

Okay. Time to be cool. Calm. Collected.

Except I'm not cool.

I'm sweating everywhere.

Pits, boobs, ass. I'm like a fountain. In the worst way.

Breathe.

When we get back to Justin's room, I'm grateful the AC is on full blast because I need it. I'm about to go stand next to it when Justin grabs my hand.

"What's up?" I croak.

"Well, I couldn't stop thinking about what you told me yesterday—your insurance not covering your surgery. It's not okay. You don't need that financial burden or extra stress. I did some research last night, and I think I might've found a solution to your problem."

My brows lift in surprise. I did plenty of researching too. Was there something I missed? There's some uncertainty in his eyes, and he looks a little sheepish. I tamp down the hope trying to blossom in my gut.

"Oh? What's that?"

He stares at me for a beat, then a calm confidence takes over, and he smiles.

"We should get married."

CHAPTER NINE

Justin

I'M worried I might've broken Jade. She's standing there blinking at me like that's the only way she can communicate.

"Married," she croaks.

Good, a word.

"I know it's a lot, but it seemed like an obvious solution."

"Obvious?"

Her voice is still high-pitched and choppy, and my confidence wanes slightly. When I came up with it, I thought I was brilliant. Then I thought about it and toned it down a smidge, but I still thought it was smart. It's a big deal, sure, but watching Jade's face right now, I'm realizing maybe the idea is a little more unhinged than I thought.

"I'm a romance narrator and you're a romance author. We both know people have gotten married in books for a lot dumber reasons than this."

"Those are... books."

"Right."

"Fiction!" she yells, turning on her heel and pacing like a caged animal.

It's a good thing we're having this conversation in private.

Still, she hasn't outright refused me, so I'm not giving up hope.

"Married!" she yells.

"Yes. Didn't we already cover that part?"

She stops and spins to face me, eyes wide. "No. We did not *cover that part.* How would that even work? We live states away from each other. Call me crazy, but I think most healthy marriages involve being in the same state, preferably the same town, and usually the same house!"

My lips pull flat. I forgot I didn't tell her *where* I was planning on moving yesterday. The conversation quickly turned to other things, and I was so focused on finding a solution to her insurance problem that I never even thought to look up how far Ida is from... what did she say? Woods Junction?

I hold my hands up as I approach her, well aware anything I say right now might spook her, and that's the last thing I want.

Fuck, I'm offering to do this to help her, but I *want* to do this. It won't just be a bruise to my ego if she says no. Another part of me will feel it too.

I rub one hand over my chest.

Why is this so important to me?

"We didn't get to talk about this yet, but I mentioned yesterday that I was planning to move."

Her brow scrunches. "You mentioned that. But you didn't mention you meant moving in with me."

Oh, I like sassy Jade.

"I was planning to move to Ida. One of my friends lives there and loves it."

"Ida? Ida, New York? As in twenty-two minutes from me?"

"Well, I didn't know that until right now, so I'll have to take your word for it, but yes. And if you don't want to do this, then that's still my plan."

She stares at me for a long moment.

"I don't even have two bedrooms," she says, like she's just realizing that for the first time. "Well, I do. But one is tiny and mostly just storage for all my books."

My stupid ass takes her lack of rebuttal as a win, and I lean into our playfulness again.

"Only one bed. One of my favorite tropes."

"I have a couch," she says flatly.

"And yet the two people almost always end up sharing a bed for some reason or another."

"Justin!" She throws her hands up in exasperation.

Dick, do not get hard right now. Do you hear me?

"I like when you say my name like that."

"Like you're clinically insane?"

But then a smile ghosts her face, and something inside me relaxes. She's going to agree to this.

"How would this work?" she asks, voice soft.

"Well, I could move in with you or you could move in with me in Ida. The apartment might be bigger—"

She shakes her head. "Maybe, but I like my apartment, and I own it. Own the building it's in. It's close to my dad, and I love Woods Junction. But I meant before that. When would we get married and would you even be able to add me to your insurance before my surgery? It's in a week."

"Well, we're in Vegas. Pretty much the city of the quickie marriage. They actually have a little chapel here at the hotel. And I already checked on the insurance stuff. I can add you right away and coverage is effective from the date we get married."

My cheeks warm, but I ignore it, watching Jade for any tiny indication of what she's thinking.

She swallows hard, then meets my eyes, her beautiful bronze ones shimmering with emotion.

"Are you sure you're okay with this? I stand to gain a lot more from it than you. You're uprooting your whole life—"

"I'm doing that anyway. Everything's packed. It's just a matter of where I ship it."

Her eyes drift to the ground. "Are you sure you want to waste your first marriage on me?"

Without thinking, I step forward and grab her chin, lifting her gaze back to me. "Nothing involving you would ever be a waste."

My heart pounds unsteadily.

Marrying her could never be a waste. But I also don't want this to be my first wedding. I want it to be my only wedding.

That's fucked, but so am I.

We're not even married yet, and I'm already catching feelings for my fake wife.

"Okay."

My gaze drifts to her soft pink lips. "Okay?"

"Yes." She pushes out of my grasp, head held high. "But we're going to write out a contract. You're doing this to help me, but I don't want to take advantage of you. I want you to get something out of this too."

She doesn't know it yet, but she's giving me more than she realizes. She's giving me a chance.

"I THINK THAT'S EVERYTHING," Jade says.

She's sitting on my bed with a Bluetooth keyboard and my tablet on her lap, typing out the few key important points she wanted to cover.

I've been standing at the end of the bed because sitting down on my bed with her seems like a bad idea. Especially for my dick.

He won't care why we're in bed together, and he'll make a mess of the situation.

"You should read over it."

She stands up and hands me the tablet, and I skim the words in the document. It's some legal form she found online that we could customize and download when we're done.

It lists the date of our marriage, then a few bullet points.

- *Bride will be added to the groom's insurance.*
- *Groom will move into bride's residence.*
- *Bride and groom will be responsible for all individual finances and share household expenses.*
- *Should the marriage end for any reason, neither party will be entitled to any assets or physical property currently held by the other party.*
- *Contract may be added to or adjusted, if needed, and re-signed by both parties.*

"Looks good to me." I pull the stylus from the holder on the side. "I think we can both sign."

She takes the tablet and the stylus from me, but pauses with her hand in the air. "Wait, we didn't put an end date on here."

"An end date?"

"Yeah. We should have an agreed upon length of time for when we'll separate and then divorce."

"No," I growl.

She leans back and stares at me, eyes narrowed. "No? Why not?"

Shit. That came too forcefully.

"I don't want to specify a timeframe because I don't want you to feel rushed. Whenever we decide is the right time, it'll be natural. It's—no hard dates. That's a deal-breaker for me."

I fold my arms over my chest like that's the end of the conversation.

She arches a perfectly sculpted brow, then smiles and shakes her head.

"Whatever you say, growly."

She quickly signs her name, then hands it to me. When I'm finished, I pass it back, and she hits a few more buttons.

"Done. I'll email you a copy."

I don't fucking need one, but whatever makes her happy.

"Okay."

"So, what comes next?"

"Chapel's already booked for Sunday morning at ten."

"You booked it before you even asked me?"

I shrug innocently. "I wasn't sure how busy it would be."

"Mhm. Sunday morning. Sunday morning? I need to find a dress! I mean, I have a couple of casual ones with me, and one nicer one, but it's black and slinky, which is not wedding vibes. I don't care if it's a quickie wedding. If it's the only one I ever end up having, I want to feel like a Disney Princess."

"A Disney Princess, huh?"

She gives me an adorable glare.

"They're where my lore started. They're the reason I'm an author. I wanted to be one. Beautiful flowers, magic animals, a library the size of a football stadium. Maybe their lives were hard at times, but they fought through and they always ended up with a man who wanted to care for them. One who would fight off monsters or his own inner demons. Being a Disney Princess is the ultimate fantasy. Life goals. Maybe this isn't my fairytale happily ever after, but I still want to feel like a fairytale princess for a day."

My heart squeezes at her words. I want her to have that fairytale wedding. I dig out my phone and search for wedding dress shops. A bunch come up within a half hour from us.

"There are a ton to choose from."

She vehemently shakes her head. "That doesn't matter. Finding a cute plus size wedding dress off the rack? That's next to impossible. Maybe I can find something online and pay to get here overnight—"

"Hold on. One of these specializes in plus size dresses and their website says they have off the rack options available in all sizes. But I'll check some of the other ones too and send you a list, so you can do that tomorrow morning. And I'll handle the rings."

Her shoulders soften. "Thank you. But shouldn't I get your ring?"

"Nope."

"But you're already—"

I pin her with a look. "Have you not realized that I'm a romantic too? This is something I want to do, so let me do it. Let me have my fun."

She gives a little headshake. "Okay. But... this is crazy. I still don't understand why you're doing all this."

Walking over to her, I pull her in for a hug, partly because I want one, but mostly because I'm hoping it'll settle her worry. That she'll remember how it feels when we touch. "Because you need help, and I want to be the one to help you. Simple as that."

She leans back and looks up at me, then smiles. "Okay."

Leaning down, I press a kiss to her forehead. "When do you need to get ready for the mixer?"

Her eyes flare and she whips her head around to look at the clock.

"Now! I need to get ready now." She pushes out of my arms and heads for the door.

"Jade?"

She turns back with her hand on the doorknob. "Yeah?"

"Wear the black dress tonight."

Her eyes widen, heat settling in them, then with a wicked smile, she leaves.

I let out a long breath and flop backward on the bed.

I am so screwed.

CHAPTER TEN

Jade

I'M in a haze as I walk into my hotel room.

When Justin said he wanted to talk, I wasn't expecting him to offer to marry me in two days.

I'm grateful. It's a huge burden off me to not have to worry about any of that financially. But at the same time... I'm getting married.

What the actual fucking fuck?

I plop down on my bed, then crawl over and grab my tablet off the bedside table.

I chew on my lip as I quickly text my dad and ask if he's up for a video call. He needs to know right now. Mostly because I need his reassurance. If he's angry or thinks this is the worst idea ever, I need to know.

I wasn't actually trying to flirt with Justin earlier when I said I'm a good girl. It's the truth. I think it's partly because I always had such an open relationship with my dad. We talked about everything, and all he ever asked of me was that I put in my best effort and always tried to make good choices. It was rare that I got in trouble, and when I did something wrong, whether I got in trouble or not, I always felt horrible about it.

Putting myself out there as an author was hard because of all the negative reviews that made me feel like I did something wrong. I finally stopped looking at them, and my mental health is better for it, but still, I don't like making mistakes or hurting others. And the last thing I ever want to do is disappoint my dad.

My phone goes off with a text from my dad saying he'd love to video chat with me, so I grab my tablet and quickly video call him.

Knots form in my stomach as he answers.

What if this is the wrong decision?

Why does the thought of it being wrong make my stomach hurt? Why do I *want* this to work out?

"Hey, kiddo."

"Hi, Dad."

His brow furrows, and he leans in toward the camera. "What's wrong?"

"Nothing exactly. Uh... okay, so this is probably going to sound crazy, so I'm just going to say it all, and then you can give me your honest thoughts."

"Okay..."

So I tell him. Everything. Except the parts about me getting off to the thought of Justin. We have the appropriate boundaries.

When I'm finished, he doesn't look angry, so that's a good sign. He's remarkably calm, actually.

"Is this something you want to do? Do you feel coerced in any way?"

"No. No coercion."

Do I want to do it? That's a tricky question to answer. Not because I don't know, but because I'm worried my dad will think I've lost it if he finds out exactly how *not* unsettled the idea makes me. It's going to be weird. And a big change. But it doesn't scare me the way it probably should. I like Justin, and even if we end up more friendly or just playing the part, the idea of sharing my life with someone—if only for a little while—is something I've been afraid to want for a long time.

"As for wanting it... I think it will be beneficial, and Justin is a good guy."

Dad stares at me for another moment, then a sly smile grows on his lips. "And is this Justin the one you've been texting?"

Shit.

My lack of answer makes his smile grow.

"Hm. I thought so. Well, you have my blessing, not that you need it."

"This is weird," I say quietly.

"What is?"

"This might be my only wedding, and you won't be here to walk me down the aisle."

Tears well in my eyes. This is stupid. It's not real.

But the marriage certificate will be. The rings and the dress will be.

"Well, sweetheart, I have a feeling that one way or another, this won't be the last wedding you have. But even if it is, know that my heart will be with you, and I'll be watching from a video call, okay?"

I sniff back my tears and nod. "Okay. I love you, Dad."

"I love you too, sweetheart."

"I need to get ready for the mixer, but I'll text you tomorrow, okay?"

"Sounds good. Have fun tonight."

"Thanks. Night, Dad."

He waves as I shut off the video call.

Leaning back against the headboard, I close my eyes for a moment.

This is crazy. I know it's crazy. But I'm a little terrified because I don't care. It feels... it feels like it did when I decided to take the leap and self-publish my first book. Utterly terrifying, but I knew it was right. I have no idea where this will lead me, but I'm not afraid to find out. I think I might be excited.

Wear the black dress tonight.

My eyes snap open again.

It might be too formal, but I don't care. I'm going to wear it and look hot as fuck.

The door between my room and Zoey and Trish's grabs my attention. But first it's time to invite my besties to a wedding.

After I knock, Zoey quickly calls for me to come in.

As soon as I'm through the door, they both stare at me.

"What happened?" Zoey asks.

I open my mouth to tell them, but all that comes out is a laugh.

They're looking at me like I'm nuts, but hey, if the shoe fits... or in my case, the wedding dress.

"Will you go shopping with me tomorrow morning? I need help. Picking a wedding dress."

"I STILL CAN'T BELIEVE you're marrying him in less than forty-eight hours," Trish whisper-squeaks in my ear as we walk into the hotel bar and lounge for the event mixer. It's only for the authors, narrators, cover models, vendors, assistants, and event staff.

Justin is standing at the bar, talking to one of the event organizers.

Thankfully, they acted fast and the creepy guy who touched my ass was removed from the event and was asked to leave the hotel this morning. Was it seriously just last night that it happened? The last twenty-four hours have been insane.

The second Justin sees me, he excuses himself from the conversation and swaggers across the room toward us.

"Damn, he's got his cover model face on," Zoey whispers. "And those sexy blue bedroom eyes are only for you."

"Hey, darlin'." He leans in and kisses my cheek. "Ladies."

Zoey and Trish both say hello, then they lock eyes and Trish smiles. "Zo and I are going to get drinks. You two have fun."

My cheeks heat a little, but I take a deep breath as Justin glances in their direction.

"I guess that means you're mine tonight," he rumbles, looking back at me.

Okay, seriously... did I write him into existence? Because *how* is he actually this swoony and sultry and just... book boyfriend ish?

"I could do worse." I keep my tone playful because playful is easy. And it keeps me from thinking too hard about the not-so-playful feelings growing in my gut for him.

He laughs and rests his hand on my low back as we walk toward the bar.

That simple touch has a fire burning inside me.

I want more. I'm terrified to admit it now, but I think I want him. *Really* want him. We're complicating what we could be by getting married in less than two days, yet I don't want to say no. I'm going to spend the next thirty-six hours praying he doesn't change his mind.

We're not even married yet, and I'm already losing the battle of not getting too attached.

But when I look up at him and find his blue eyes already fixed on me, I don't think I'm the only one.

CHAPTER ELEVEN

Justin

TODAY'S THE DAY. And as I sit in bed, tablet in hand, getting ready to make an important video call, I'm nervous. These two are my family, and I hope they take it okay.

Before I can hit the button to call them, they call me. That's what I get for texting to make sure they were free for one right now.

I swipe to answer and am greeted with Devon's and Kennedy's very serious faces.

"Doesn't look like you're in jail," Devon says.

"Why would I video call you from jail? How would I do that?"

Dev shrugs. "I don't know. You're the one being weird and formal."

"Is everything okay?" Kennedy asks.

I blow out a breath and run a hand through my hair.

"Everything's good. I'm just calling to update you about a life change."

Kennedy's eyes narrow. "Are you doing porn? Seriously, tell me the truth, and tell me which websites to avoid, because—no offense—I don't want to see that."

The way her lips tip up at the corners tells me she's fucking with me.

"I'm not doing porn," I say flatly.

"Then what's up? Have you been body snatched? Abducted by aliens? Stop being weird," Devon says.

"I'm getting married."

Kennedy's eyes fly wide, and Devon just stares.

Glancing at her boyfriend, Kend grabs the phone and tilts it toward her. "When and to who? What haven't you told us?"

I clear my throat. "I am marrying Jade."

"Jade..." Kennedy's eyes get even wider. "Jade Jackson? The author that you... damn. That's fast." She points at me. "Did you knock her up?"

That gets a laugh out of me. "Sorry. Surprise pregnancy isn't my trope."

"You're right, it's he falls first." She tilts her head. "And hard. You really like her."

"I do."

Devon appears in the frame again. "But this is fast. If you tell us it's right, we'll support you, no questions asked. As your best friend, it's my job to ask... are you sure?"

I stare at them through the screen. "I'm sure, but there's more you should know. He falls first isn't my only trope."

Then I explain it all.

"Okay, you have my stamp of approval," Devon says when I've finished. "This is so you it hurts. And after all we talked about when you were here last month, I know this is ultimately what you want. I trust your judgment that she's it."

"You're writing your own love story," Kennedy says. "And you deserve that. Also, you should totally write an actual story based on this one day.”

I laugh to myself. “We’ll see how this plays out first.”

Kennedy meets my eyes. “It’s going to be perfect.”

“What time is this happening?” Devon asks.

“Uh, just under two hours. Why?”

“I want to be sure we have time to call Gladys and my parents so we can all be on a video call to watch.”

Emotion swells in my chest, and for a second, it’s hard to talk. Dev’s parents have always treated me like a second son, and Gladys, who has run Devon’s family’s inn for most of his life, has always been a mix of mom and aunt to me.

“Thank you.”

“I wish I was there to hug you,” Kennedy says.

“Well, you’ll have to come out and visit. Did I mention she lives twenty minutes from Frannie?”

“Almost like it was meant to be,” Devon says knowingly.

“Hey, you remember what you told me when you were here visiting? That I was happier here in Brighton than you’d ever seen me?” Kennedy asks. I nod, and she smiles. “You’re happier than I’ve ever seen you.”

“Thanks, Kend.”

There’s a knock on the door, and I glance over at it. Standing up, I bring my tablet with me. Hopefully it’s not Jade changing her mind or Zoey or Trish coming to tell me she ran off.

Breathe.

I swing the door open and find a man who looks familiar, but I can’t place why.

“Hi. Can I help you?”

“You’re Justin Ayers?”

And something about the sound of his voice and the look in his eyes tells me exactly who it is.

I look back down at the tablet to see Kennedy and Devon staring back at me questioningly. “Guys, I’ve gotta go.”

I'M STANDING in the hallway, waiting anxiously for Jade. The little chapel is set up perfectly, and I really hope she's going to love it. Zoey and Trish are already inside, along with the minister.

Devon, Kennedy, Gladys, and Devon's parents are all at the inn, ready to watch this on the large TV in the ballroom. Their support means more to me than anything my parents could ever give me.

I already know my folks are going to be pissed and they'll guilt trip me six ways from Sunday, but I don't need their approval. I paid my landlord an extra month's rent for him to relabel all my boxes and be there when the shipping company comes to pick them up, so I don't have to bother going home.

Not home. Not anymore.

I'm almost afraid to hope that Woods Junction will feel like home, but I'm optimistic. I'm always optimistic. It's what gets me through life. But acknowledging how badly I want this is risking my heart getting crushed.

I never thought I could be sure of something so quickly, but I'm sure about Jade, and I know this is the path I'm meant to be on.

The sound of footsteps makes me look up, and when I do, my breath sticks in my lungs. There, walking down the hallway, is Jade looking utterly breathtaking in a short tank top dress with a flared tulle bottom. Her hair is swept back into a low bun with side braids, wispy strands framing her face, and she's smiling. It's a soft, comfortable smile that makes my heart race.

"Hi, almost-hubby."

"Hi. You are... stunning. Captivating. Mesmerizing. I need more synonyms because those don't do you justice."

She laughs a little. "Thank you. You look very handsome."

I feel like nothing compared to her. My light gray suit and

crisp white shirt are fine, but she looks like she stepped out of a whimsical love story.

I hope the little chapel does her justice.

She steps up to me and takes my hand. "Ready for this? Last chance to run."

"Not a chance, darlin'. I'm a lucky man."

Her cheeks heat, and when she looks into my eyes, that same heat dances in her brown irises.

"I'm the perfect representation of a princess today. Pretty dress, in a bit of pinch, and need a little help. That's when the handsome prince strolls in and offers her his hand."

"It's an honor to be your prince."

Her gaze flits to my lips, and I find myself reaching for her, wrapping a hand around the side of her neck, my stomach buzzing with desire as she inches closer. I've wanted this since the moment we met. Wanted her lips on mine. Wanted to feel the amplification of this connection between us.

"Justin," she breathes against my lips.

The sound of a door slamming down the hall makes us jump.

She sucks in a big breath and takes half a step back. "I don't think we're supposed to kiss until *after* the ceremony."

"Is that a promise?"

Her eyes flash with mischief. "It wouldn't be a fairytale wedding if it didn't have a magical kiss."

She runs her hand over my arm as she goes to move past me, but I step in front of her again.

"Before you go in there, there's someone special who wants to see you."

Her brow furrows. "Who?"

I knock twice on the door, and slowly, it opens.

I watch as Jade's face goes from confused to surprised to brimming with emotion.

"Dad?"

CHAPTER TWELVE

Jade

"HI, SWEETHEART."

"I'll give you two a minute." Justin pats my dad's shoulder as he walks back into the chapel.

"What are you doing here?" I choke out.

"I wasn't going to miss my little girl's wedding day."

"Even if it's not—"

"Don't say it isn't real, Jade. You're in a beautiful dress, and that man couldn't hide the way he feels for you if he tried. Maybe it's not how you thought it would be. Maybe it's for different reasons, but it's still real, and you should enjoy every second."

The thing is, this is what I imagined. Maybe not the location or the reasoning, but the dress, the way Justin smiles at me, the comfort I feel, and the whimsical romantic vibes are everything I ever would've wanted for my wedding.

I second-guess things. I always have. It's part of that *good girl* side of me. I want to be sure I'm making the right decision, but I don't want to second-guess this. I don't want to overthink this. All I want is to be happy today.

"You really got on a plane and flew out here?"

"I did. I got in early this morning and went right to Justin's room. With a little help from Zoey. She gave me his room number."

I throw my arms around him. "Thank you. Doing this without you... never would've felt right. Whatever happens, I want to look back and remember you walking me down the aisle. I love you, Dad."

"I love you too, sweetheart."

I step back, and he smiles as he takes me in.

"You look beautiful."

"Thank you. I feel beautiful."

"You should."

"Hey, you didn't mention this to Mom, did you?"

He shakes his head. "Definitely not. When will you tell her?"

"I don't know. Probably tonight or tomorrow. You know how she is. I don't want her thoughts or for her to nitpick at me today. Even though she'll have something to say regardless."

"Well, let it flow in one ear and out the other. She doesn't define you. You define yourself."

I smile at that. I am who I am because of how my dad raised me.

"Today, I'm a princess living my fairytale."

"It's an honor to be a part of it." He holds out his elbow to me. "Shall we?"

"Let's do it."

He pulls open one of the chapel's double doors, and as we walk inside, my mouth drops.

I'm not sure what I was expecting, but I wasn't expecting this.

It's a small room with a few rows of white chairs. The walls and ceiling are covered with tulle curtains, making it feel bigger and more upscale—and taking away any sense that you're in a hotel. Warm white strand lights add a lovely ambience to the room. But it's the large detail that has nothing to do with the hotel and everything to do with Justin that makes me tear up.

At the front of the aisle isn't a typical altar or wedding arch. No. It's the beautiful book arch from the signing. Now with added string lights, tulle, and flowers.

It's my real world and my dream life colliding.

Justin stands in front of the book arch smiling at me, and I'm swept away in the whimsy of the moment and the peace in my heart.

I won't just be happy if this is the only wedding I'll ever get. I *hope* this is the only wedding I'll ever have. Because nothing else could compare. And I'm starting to think no one else could ever compare to Justin.

"Are we ready?" the minister—or justice of the peace—asks.

Justin's piercing gaze lands on me, and I nod.

Dad squeezes my arm.

This is all so strangely anti-climactic.

I thought I'd be nervous, but I'm calm.

Somewhere deep inside, I know this is the right decision, even if where it might lead is still unclear.

Justin watches every step, a huge smile on his face.

He's such a golden retriever. Always happy—and he wants to make me happy.

Dad stops at the last row of chairs and takes my hands. "I'm proud of you, kiddo." Then he kisses my cheek and turns to Justin. "Take care of her."

There's a surprising amount of emotion in Justin's voice when he says, "I will."

My stomach whirls.

There's the anticipation and excitement I was looking for. And as I step in front of Justin and he takes my hands, I know I'll remember everything about this moment forever.

The book arch looms beside us, more beautiful than I could've imagined.

This is perfect. If anything, it's a shame the chapel is empty.

The minister starts speaking, and though I try to focus on his words, they're more like background noise. My mind wanders, thinking of what comes next. Of going home. Being married.

"Love is born in seconds, but grows over a lifetime."

The minister's words—*my* words, from one of my books—draw me back to the moment. When I look at Justin, he gives me that boyish smile.

"What can I say? I'm a fan."

The minister goes on, spinning off that quote into how love can grow and change over time and how important it is to help facilitate that growth. But I'm focused on Justin. The way he looks at me.

I don't know that there's been a magical blossom of love between us, but... I'd be lying if I said I wasn't hoping we planted the seeds. Or are planting them. I want a chance—a *real* chance.

We say our simple one-line vows, then it's time for the rings.

Zoey brings over two boxes and hands one to each of us.

I go first, admiring the beveled gray tungsten carbide ring as I slip it on his finger. A little thrill runs through me. A wedding band signifying that he's mine, even if it's only on paper.

I hold my hand out as Justin opens the ring box, and as he slips it on my finger, my jaw drops. I've never seen another ring like it. It's an oval diamond with a halo of diamonds around it. Then on the sides near the top and bottom are a total of four small diamonds. The setting rises around it almost making it look like a magic mirror. It's all set on a yellow gold band, which also has a few diamonds along the sides of the setting. It's gorgeous, but for me, it's more than just a pretty ring, and when I meet Justin's eyes, it's clear he knows that.

It's my princess ring.

And Justin, with his bright blue eyes, golden blond hair, and boyish charm, is my prince charming.

"I now pronounce you husband and wife. You may kiss the bride."

Justin eagerly steps forward and wraps his hand around the

side of my neck, dipping his head and slanting his mouth over mine.

I inhale sharply at the burst of electricity, a tingly feeling that rushes through my entire body.

Grabbing his arm, I pull him closer, desperate for more.

His tongue traces across the seam of my lips, and I open for him. The second our tongues twist together, I'm lost in a state of bliss. Nothing has ever been more right. One hand moves down his chest, and all I want to do is untuck his shirt, feel his skin, and—

I remember where we are at the same time he does, and we slowly untangle.

He takes my hand and faces me forward so we can walk down the aisle. My cheeks are flushed, and the color only deepens when he leans in and whispers, "Magical enough?"

I bite my lip as we walk down the aisle. Trish is staring at us with one brow cocked while Zoey smirks to herself as she claps. I can't even look at my dad.

That wasn't just a kiss. It was a kiss that wanted to start things. Create things. Change things. Magic doesn't begin to describe it.

But because playful is our go-to, I smile up at him and say, "It'll do."

And it will. It'll do all kinds of things to me, my body... my heart.

In case it wasn't clear, I'm screwed. We've been married for less than five minutes, and I'm already falling for my husband.

CHAPTER THIRTEEN

Justin

MY PHONE HASN'T STOPPED GOING off the entire drive from the airport to Woods Junction. After a whirlwind of a day, we're almost back to Jade's house. We took a few photos and had a champagne toast after the wedding, then went right to our hotel rooms, changed and packed up, then left for the airport. I surprised Jade with first-class seats since I had to book a flight for myself anyway. Now, it's just after seven at night, and we're both exhausted, but we should be there any minute.

And the group chat has been keeping me entertained. I might've been a chaos gremlin and sent a text to the friend group right before I got on the plane and wouldn't be able to answer.

It was entertaining when I finally got off the plane.

I laugh out loud when I read the latest message.

"What now?" Jade asks with a smile.

"Frannie wants to know if I married you just so I could get

spoilers for the rest of the Marianos series." I side-eye her. "Do I get spoilers?"

Jade's smile morphs into something much more troublemaking. "If you wanted spoilers, you should've put it in the contract."

"That's just mean."

She winks at me, then puts her turn signal on, visibly relaxing as she pulls into the driveway.

"Well, here we are. This is home."

Jade pulls the car to a stop and lets out a long breath.

"It's bigger than I thought it would be."

It's a big square-ish house, with the top floor a bit smaller than the bottom. When she described the two-story setup, I imagined it might be small or cramped, but from the outside, it looks spacious.

"Yeah, it's not bad." She yawns and stretches as she climbs out of the car.

I grab our bags from the trunk and swat her hand away when she tries to take hers.

"Let me do husbandly things."

She laughs and shakes her head. "Whatever you want."

She leads the way to the side of the house, and we take the stairs up to the second floor. When she swings the door open, I'm hit with a wave of warmth. Not physically. The air conditioning is running, and it's nice and cool. It's an emotional sensation. Peaceful.

"This is it," she says. "Not huge, but it's cozy."

"It's comfortable. And I mean that in the best possible way. It's a home, not a house."

It's almost like I've been here before, though outside of the city, I've never explored New York. It's familiar. Like coming home. The word settles in my gut and the warmth I felt when I walked in spreads.

"Glad you think so. You're stuck with it." She looks around. "It's a lot nicer than when I bought it. The structure was good, and I love the location, but the inside was a mess. My dad and a couple of his contractor friends—one of whom lives downstairs—helped fix it up." She moves through the apartment, turning lights on, though I stay planted in the entryway portion of the living room, taking it all in. "And by helped, I mean they did all the work while I gave them ideas."

The living room is open to the kitchen and dining area, which is a good size.

"Was it a two-family when you bought it?"

"Yeah, but there were still stairs inside connecting the two floors. About where you're standing, actually. My dad blocked it off, but made sure it was easily reversible if I ever wanted to turn it back into a single-family home."

Slipping my shoes off, I follow her into the apartment. She has a massive L-shaped couch that takes up most of the living room. There's also a large rectangular coffee table, a TV stand with a built-in bookcase, and another tall bookcase to the side.

"Your dad used to be a contractor?" I ask, walking past the dining table and around the counter into the kitchen, where Jade is sitting.

"Yeah, he was hurt in a forklift accident when I was young and pivoted to working with accessibility in contracting. It's strange to say, but I think it worked out better for him. It was a long recovery, and he still has some mobility issues, but he loves his life. He also runs a YouTube cooking channel." She shrugs. "He's never been the type to let anything hold him back, and he's always encouraged me to live the same way."

"He seems awesome. We didn't talk for too long this morning, but it's clear how much he cares for you, and also how much he respects you. I'm glad he was there for you today."

Jade beams at that.

"I'm glad he came too. I was... a little upset on Friday at the thought of him not being there."

"I wish you would've told me. I would've called and talked to him about it—"

She waves a hand dismissively, then fills a cup with water from the fridge and hands it to me.

"You didn't need to. And it all worked out okay."

"What about your mom?"

She snorts at that. "I'll tell her. Soon. Ish. I don't know. Let's just say I'm glad she wasn't there. She would've been saying things like *are you sure about that dress?* Or *really, the book arch?* Or telling me to wear different shoes or criticizing my makeup, saying my dress was too short." Her voice drops. "Or making a comment about my weight."

"What?" I growl. Because fuck anyone who thinks they should comment on anyone else's weight, *ever*.

Jade sighs and hoists herself onto the counter. "My mom wanted the tiny, pretty, popular girl, and she got me. She's always had some sort of critique, but honestly, who cares? She was too busy flitting around the world on her 'wellness' adventures with her boyfriend of the moment to actually raise me, so her thoughts don't mean much to me. They're mostly just annoying. She didn't actually want a child. She wanted a human doll she could dress pretty and control. That's not me. I've never been good at fitting in the boxes people say I should fit into."

I set my glass down and walk over to her, cupping her cheeks.

"And you never should. Take up space and don't take anyone's shit."

She breathes in heavily, eyes locked on mine.

The world around us seems to slow down and go blurry. There's only the two of us and the sparks of our connection.

She licks her lips, and reality tries to push its way in.

I don't know what I'm doing. I don't know what *we're* doing. We kissed this morning, and it was fucking incredible, but does that mean we're kissing now? Is it a thing? I don't know.

So, almost painfully, I drop my hands and take a step back.

After a long moment, Jade slides off the counter. "Want a tour?"

"Yeah. Show me the digs."

The digs? What is wrong with me?

It seems to knock some of the tension out of her shoulders, though, so I roll with it and follow her out of the kitchen.

"This is the hallway. Very exciting. And on the right, we have the bathroom. It's massive, and it has two doors. One to the hall and one to my bedroom. So make sure you lock the applicable one when you're using it. Come on. We'll cut through."

She leads me through the bathroom, opening cabinets to point out where towels and toiletries are, then pulls open the other door into her bedroom.

"This is my room and writing sanctuary."

It's a big room with plush beige carpeting, a king-size bed, and two windows on the far wall. A desk sits in the corner near one of them. The other has an air conditioning unit in it. Weird, because I'm pretty sure there's central AC, but whatever. I think she told me once she'd never survive in the heat of the south, so maybe that's why.

Either way, as I walk through the space, I can't help but hope I'll be lucky enough to earn an invitation to this room one day.

We end up in the hallway again. Then she opens the door across the hall, revealing a much smaller room.

"I know you said you'll need a place to record, and this should work. We'll have to move a couple of my bookcases—or better yet, finally get some good shelving for the closet I don't use so I can store most of my books in there. The only thing I really need in here is my book packaging station in the corner."

"This should definitely work. Thanks."

She laughs a little. "It's the least I can do."

We walk back down the hall and she points to the two closets —one for cleaning and house supplies, the other for linens.

She grabs sheets and blankets from the linen closet and we head back to the living room.

"I promise the couch is super comfy."

"I believe you," I say gently. The last thing I want is for her to feel awkward or uncomfortable about any of this.

"Okay, well, uh..." She sighs. "I feel gross. Okay if I shower?"

"As long as I get to shower after you."

"Actually, you go first, and I'll unpack while you do that. Just open the door from the bathroom to my bedroom when you're done. And if you need to unpack anything, you can put it in the closet in the book room."

"If you're sure."

"Yeah, go ahead."

"Thanks."

She nods, and we stare at each other for a moment, then I squeeze her hand and aim for the shower.

I'M in the kitchen warming up lasagna Papa Jackson left in the fridge when Jade walks in, hair wet and looking much more relaxed in an oversized tee and sexy little booty shorts.

I nod at her shirt. "Han Solo, huh?"

She looks down, then back up at me, biting her lip. "Yeah. I love the original *Star Wars* movies and he was my first crush."

"Harrison Ford?"

She looks horrified by the thought. "No. Han Solo. Ageless fictional character. Harrison Ford is older than my dad."

I chuckle at that and pull the plate of lasagna from the microwave.

"Not an age gap girl?"

"Not that big of one. Unless it's a five-hundred-year-old fae, but I'm okay with that because they still look and act like a twenty-five to thirty-year-old and if they're immortal or semi-immortal, that's kind of their thirty."

"Fair enough. Ready to eat?"

"So ready."

The toaster oven goes off and she smiles happily. "He made garlic bread too?"

"Yep."

Once we've filled our plates, we get settled on the couch, and as we do, both of our phones go off. And then go off several more times.

Right. I might've been a chaos gremlin again and created a group chat for the Baker Girls Book Club.

Jade looks at me questioningly as we both reach for our phones.

I open my texts and immediately laugh.

KENNEDY

Is this the text where we finally get to yell at Jade?

KENNEDY

Since I'm not as creepy as Justin and didn't want to slide into her DMs.

KENNEDY

Anyway... Jade... HOW DARE YOU?

HALLIE

She woke up and chose violence. It's the only answer for the ending to book 7.

HARDY

La la la. I can't hear you. I haven't finished yet! No spoilers!

HALLIE

Get out of the chat then. We have grievances to air.

FRANNIE

I'm not ready yet, but that's my own doing. I know the last two chapters are going to destroy me, so I'm avoiding them and having a Joey Tribbiani moment.

KENNEDY

Put the book in the freezer?

FRANNIE

Metaphorically speaking since I'm reading the
e-books.

HARDY

Seriously! No spoilers. I'm muting this chat
until I'm done!

Jade, welcome to chaos.

"What did you do?" she asks with a laugh.

I shrug innocently, but she doesn't buy it. She shakes her head and types out a response.

JADE

I don't know who all of you are yet, but
welcome to the party. I provide tissues and
emotional support cat memes. You can send
me your therapy bills, but don't expect me to
pay them. 🥹

JADE

Oh, and I only have brunch with Satan the
second Tuesday of every month. And yes, we
do use your tears to brew the tea. XO

I laugh as I read the texts.

"You're savage. I kinda like it."

Her eyes dance, and it's impossible to miss the shift in the air around us. If we lock eyes for longer than a second, the tension between us grows exponentially.

After a moment, she rolls her eyes and smiles. "I like having fun with it. And obviously, it's different with your friends, but generally speaking, being playful creates a stronger barrier between my work life and my personal life. They can bleed together, and I try to keep that from happening too much. You somehow got through."

"I'm sneaky like that."

"So, who all is on this text with us?"

"First one is Kennedy."

"One of your besties."

"Yep. And second is Hallie."

"Her younger cousin and Frannie's sister?"

"Yes. And Frannie was the fourth one. The third is Hardy."

"Hardy?" she asks in confusion.

"Well, Ryan, but that's what he goes by—"

"Wait. Ryan? As in Ryan Hardison? The New York Bandits wide receiver?"

"Little bit. Are you a Bandits fan?"

"I'm a sports girl in general, but yeah, my dad and I always watched their games together—sometimes still do. We even went to a game their opening season... twelve or thirteen years ago, I think?" She shakes her head in disbelief, then her brow furrows as she puts the rest of it together. "Wait. And Frannie's boyfriend Mark is Mark Abbott? Their quarterback? The one who went through that whole scandal thing and then maybe got engaged— was it Frannie? Are they engaged?"

I laugh out loud at the rapid-fire pace she spits all that out.

"They're not engaged. Mark just apologized to her in the dumbest way possible. They'd only known each other for like a week at that point."

She side-eyes me, then gestures between the two of us.

"Hey, we'd at least been talking for *two* weeks."

"Oh, I'm sorry. You're right. Big difference." She shakes her head. "Wait. Was Hardy one of the guys you messaged me about the other week?"

"Maybe."

She grabs my arm. "I'll never mention it. I was just curious. And I'll be paying attention now. I'm invested." She sets her phone to the side and sighs. "I'm also exhausted. And hungry."

"Eat, darlin'."

"Want to watch something?"

"Sure. What are you in the mood for?"

She shrugs. "I don't know. What's your go-to show?"

"*The Mandalorian.*" I glance at her shirt again. "I'm kind of a *Star Wars* nerd."

She smiles at that. "How much of one?"

"You know how you said Disney Princesses were your lore? *Star Wars* is mine. I've watched every iteration of it. While I didn't love all the later movies, I still love the universe, and they've done a phenomenal job with some of the shows. *The Mandalorian* just happens to be a favorite."

"Let's watch it then."

"Have you seen it?"

She shakes her head and grabs the remote. "Nope. So I'm expecting you to pause it and explain all the details to me. Give me the lore and behind-the-scenes info."

I blink at her a couple of times, surprised by the emotion that swells in me. "Really?"

"Yeah. I love finding out the background of things and catching all the little Easter eggs, so explain away. Plus, it's a fun way to get to know you better, seeing you enjoy something and share your love of it."

Well, damn. Hit me right in the feels.

"Okay. But on one condition. You have to do the same with your favorite show or movie or universe."

"*Once Upon a Time.*"

I chuckle. "That tracks."

"Have you seen it?"

"Nope."

"Okay, then. One episode of your show and one episode of mine each night."

"Sounds perfect."

I shift a little closer, then finally take a bite of my lasagna and nearly groan.

"Good, right?"

I nod. "Amazing."

"Get used to it. Dad loves to share his cooking."

I glance at her, only to see her eyes fixed on the beginning of the episode.

"I can definitely get used to this."

But I'm not talking about her dad's cooking. I'm talking about *this*. Sitting on the couch, watching my favorite show with the girl I'm falling for.

It hasn't been long, but I can't shake the feeling I've finally found the home I've been looking for. Not the apartment, but the incredible woman by my side.

CHAPTER FOURTEEN

Jade

I NEED to get out of bed.

Everything was cozy and peaceful until I woke up, looked down at my hand, and remembered I'm married.

Not that it's a bad thing, but... there's someone else in my apartment.

Other than Zoey and Trish staying over on occasion after a little too much wine, I've never woken up to someone else being in my space.

I don't know what to do or what to say. Is he a night owl or an early riser? Am I going to be disturbing his routine? Are we going to chat or pass by each other like ships in the night?

Maybe I should get up and figure it out.

How shocking that I'm overthinking this.

With a deep breath, I force myself out of the bed and throw on a cute cropped tee and some thick biker-style shorts.

I open my door quietly and try to avoid the squeaky spots in the hallway in case Justin is sleeping, but when I get out there, I find him in the kitchen, looking through the refrigerator.

"Morning."

He closes the door and smiles at me. "Morning, darlin'."

We stare at each other for a moment, and the awkwardness in my gut makes my skin crawl.

"Sleep okay?" I ask, but it comes out squeaky.

His smile grows. "Great. That's a comfortable couch."

"It is," I agree.

But when he turns his back to me and heads for the coffeepot, I frown.

I didn't think a second of this through—actually living with him. We're going to be married for at least six months. Will he sleep on the couch the entire time? That seems weird.

And terrible to ask of him. Maybe it's comfortable for a few nights, but six months? He deserves better than that.

Maybe we could squeeze a twin bed in the extra room. Not much, but it would be better than the couch.

Is it wrong that I wouldn't mind having him in my bed? A wife wanting to sleep next to her husband... crazy, right?

"How strong do you like your coffee?"

My gaze snaps to Justin, and I relax a little. Figure out the logistics later.

"Lorelai Gilmore strong."

He grins at me. "My kind of girl."

Am I? Could I be? We have chemistry, there's no denying that. And he's one of the sweetest people I've ever known. He's willing to do a lot to make me happy, but does that mean... we could be something?

Everything has been so upside down and backward that I don't know what I'm doing or thinking.

But I know I like being around him, so I need to chill out and focus on that.

"I was thinking of making some pancakes. Sound good?" he asks.

My brow furrows and I open the refrigerator, surprised to find it stocked with food.

"Did you go shopping?" I ask, confused.

He chuckles and hands me a Post-it.

"Apparently, Papa Jackson was busy before he flew out to Vegas."

Jade,
Figured you'd need some food in your fridge when you got home.
Love ya.
Dad

That's Dad. Always going several steps above and beyond. Flying out to Vegas to surprise me? Cool, just a quick stop at the store to stock my fridge first.

My mom was an absentee parent at best, but my dad more than made up for it.

I turn back to Justin. "Pancakes sound great. Interested in an omelet on the side?"

"Sounds delicious."

He starts opening cabinets and looking around for the mixing bowls. I almost tell him where they are, but I kind of like the look of him bending over and rummaging through the cabinets. It's almost like he belongs here.

Plus, the way he smiles when he finds what he's looking for is utterly adorable.

"Okay if I put on some music?"

He turns and looks at me with an amused smirk. "Why wouldn't it be?"

"I don't know. Maybe you're one of those people who likes to do things in complete silence."

He laughs as he spins the lazy Susan and pulls out some of the dry ingredients for pancakes. "Definitely not."

I connect my phone to the Bluetooth speaker, then pause again.

"Any requests?"

He shrugs. "Whatever you want."

I scoff at that. "If I pick, it'll be all Taylor Swift."

"I don't care." He squints at me. "Should I care?"

"No. I just want to be considerate of what you like."

"Listen to what you enjoy, Jade. I'm not here to control you. Just like with watching TV shows together, I want to know what music you enjoy. What songs bring you to life. Plus, I'm man enough to admit that I love Queen Tay Tay. So put it on."

I swallow hard. "Okay."

I settle on a playlist of some of my favorite Taylor Swift songs, then go back to the fridge and pull out the eggs and cheese.

"You like veggies in your omelet?" I ask.

Dad really stocked the fridge. There are mushrooms, peppers, onions, asparagus, and fresh spinach.

"Sure. I'm a kitchen sink kinda guy. Throw it all in."

"I can do that."

We settle in, Justin making pancakes and me prepping the omelet.

This was a stupid job for me though, because holding a knife is one of those fun tasks that makes my hand tingly, achy, and numb.

Which must be why I keep stopping and sneaking glances at Justin.

He occasionally whisper-sings along with the words and is constantly bouncing back and forth or even dancing.

God, why does everything he do make me feel all... swoony?

I'm a swooning mess over my husband.

Fake husband.

I think.

At this point, I know less than Jon Snow.

Turning back to the cutting board in front of me, I get back to it, hating the ache that quickly builds.

When Justin starts singing along with *Love Story*, my eyes are instantly drawn to him again.

A little too drawn to him.

"Shit."

The knife clatters to the cutting board as my heartbeat pounds in my ears. Almost sliced my fingertip off because I was looking at Justin and not at what I was cutting.

Could I blame my carpal tunnel? Probably. But it would be a lie.

Justin's at my side in a second. "Are you okay?"

I nod. "Yeah. The knife just slipped. I'm good."

But he doesn't seem to believe me, because he takes my hand in his and looks it over carefully.

My hand tingles being wrapped in his. As if my body's on autopilot, I move closer.

His gaze goes from my hand to my face, and he stares at me for a moment, my hand still cupped in his.

"It looks okay."

Swallowing hard, I nod, eyes still locked on him as Taylor Swift boisterously tells us we should say yes... to whatever this is between us.

His Adam's apple bobs and he steps back, letting my hand slowly drop.

"Be careful. Don't need you cutting off any fingers now. Those hands need to stay intact."

I give a little nod and a small smile as he turns back to the stove.

But all I can think is that I want his presence back. I want his attention on me again.

Falling for him might be a risk, but not falling for him seems like an impossibility.

"CAN I guess who Evvie ends up with?"

"No. No spoilers. But I guess... you can read book eight."

His eyes light up. "Really?"

"Yes. I'd love to be able to talk about it with you, but I want to see your reaction as you read it first. Unspoiled."

"Scouts honor. I won't read ahead."

We're still sitting at the kitchen table, though our plates and mugs are empty. We've just been talking. Not about anything big, but lots of little things. An easy conversation.

"I like the idea of having someone to talk about it all with. I mean, I have Zoey and Trish, but it's different. You're... here. God, that sounds so stupid."

He reaches across the table and rests his hand over mine, and there's that tingly feeling again. Like sparks bursting out of my hand and dancing up my arm.

"It doesn't sound stupid. You want someone to share your art with in a personal way. Not because of the art itself, but because of how it makes you feel."

I stare at him because that's all I can do. He's exactly right.

I don't want to share it with him as an author to another author or reader. I want to share it with him as my partner.

On paper, that's what we are, but in reality... I have no idea what we're doing.

But with his hand on mine and his eyes filled with tenderness, it's hard not to see flashes of what we *could* be.

JUSTIN TURNS off the TV after our episode of *Once Upon a Time.*

We watched *The Mandalorian* first, and I'm really enjoying it so far. It's got just enough of the classic *Star Wars* vibes I like while still being its own interesting, unique story.

"What do you think so far?"

"When do Snow and Charming find each other again? When does the curse get broken? Who hurt Regina? I need to know all the things."

I give him a sweet smile. "Sorry. My no spoilers rule extends beyond my books."

He groans. "Fine. But next rainy day, I foresee a binge watch."

"I won't complain."

"Hopefully not too soon though. I want to enjoy that park more. It's beautiful."

"It is." We went for a walk around it today, then drove around the tiny town portion of Woods Junction. "On the far side of the park, there are a few more walking trails. And the other end actually has a little path that connects it to the main part of town."

"That's would be cool. I'd love to explore the town more. Really get to know it."

"Do you like it so far?"

I don't know why I'm desperate for the answer to be yes. He was planning to move to Ida, and when all is said and done, that's probably where he'll end up.

"Yeah, I do. The coffee and bookstore you took me to was cute, and the people were friendly. I want to go full Gilmore Girls and immerse myself in the town, though. Go for a walk, chat with people, maybe stop by that tiny diner."

"We could go there for breakfast tomorrow. The walking path leads right there."

"That would be awesome."

I smile at him, but it quickly turns into a yawn.

"You should get some sleep." Then he catches my yawn. "I should too."

"Right. And I'm sitting on your bed."

I hop up, cringing at how that sounded.

Glancing at the couch, my heart lurches. *Seriously, how long do I make him sleep there?*

What's the alternative?

I hate this uncertainty and how weird it makes me feel.

I throw my thumb over my shoulder. "Let me know if you need anything."

He's already making up his bed on the couch.

"Will do."

I stand there awkwardly, staring at him.

"Well... I, uh... sleep well. Goodnight."

Then I turn and scurry toward my bedroom as he calls after me. "Goodnight."

Once in the safety of my bedroom, I collapse on my bed and rub my hands over my face.

Why did no one warn me that a marriage of convenience isn't always convenient? Sometimes it's weird, complicated, and downright awkward, and that's leaving out the tension that forms every time we're in a room together.

I'm not sure if I want to kiss him or jump him or declare him mine forever. But I'm certain if we keep going like this, one way or another, that tension between us is going to keep growing until it explodes.

CHAPTER FIFTEEN

Justin

THE AIR CONDITIONING isn't cold enough.

That or I've been working too hard.

Or, it might be my wife standing a few feet away in a sports bra and workout shorts while she hums along with whatever she's listening to.

Her back lightly glistens with sweat, and I run a hand down my own sweaty chest.

She was working out in her bedroom while I was reorganizing some things in the extra room, so I can build my recording space.

Now she's standing in front of the blender, completely unaware of my presence.

Creeper, party of one.

But she's my wife. I'm supposed to creep on her, right?

Fake wife.

But I don't want her to be. I don't want a second of this to be fake. I don't consider it fake. Now, it's just a matter of convincing

Jade. Maybe if I lean into our playfulness, the tension will finally spill over and we'll take a step forward.

I'll take anything I can get. Just having her lips on mine again would be heaven.

As she puts the cap back on the milk, I make my way over to her, wrap my arm around her waist, and pluck one of her earbuds out and put it in my ear.

"What are we listening to?"

But as I get the earbud situated in my ear, I get the answer.

A *very* dirty song.

That Ludacris one. *What's Your Fantasy?*

Jade turns to gape at me, horrified.

"Damn, darlin'."

She gives my chest a shove. "Rude. You don't just sneak up on people! Or steal their headphones!"

She pulls the earbud out of my ear while taking the other out of hers and setting them both down.

I brush my thumb over her cheek. "Are you blushing?"

"No," she huffs.

"Mhm. There's nothing to be embarrassed about. We all have fantasies. Want to tell me about yours?"

She spins back around and pins me with what I'm learning is her signature "pissed off Jade" look. Part playfulness, mostly *I'm-going-to-cut-you*.

"I'll tell you mine if you tell me yours," she purrs. But it almost sounds murdery.

I take her in. Pissed off Jade really turns me on. Thankfully, my cargo shorts hide my semi.

Dragging my teeth over my bottom lip, I lean in. "Nah. I already know what yours is."

She rolls her shimmering brown eyes. "Oh, really?"

"Yep. In the library, right? Maybe on some books?" I wiggle my eyebrows as I reference one of the places in the song.

She stares at me for a long beat, then the hint of a smirk

appears. "And defile a sacred space? Maybe. But I can't promise I'd be quiet."

She says the last part just loud enough for me to hear—another reference to the song. But damn if I don't love how she plays with me.

"I wouldn't complain, darlin'. Now, since I've been an ass and interrupted your smoothie-making, how about you let me finish up?"

She quirks a brow. "I can make a smoothie."

"Never said you couldn't. Just want to say I'm sorry."

She opens her mouth to respond, but before she can, her phone rings.

"Ah, saved by bell. You answer that, and I'll finish up here."

She shakes her head, but grabs her phone. "Fine."

But as she walks away, she makes a little *ugh* noise.

I add a pinch of salt—a secret ingredient that brings out the other flavors, even in something sweet—and a dash of vanilla, then add some more frozen berries and milk and blend it all up.

Once I'm finished, I pour some into glasses for Jade and me, but before I can go find her, she reappears, hand wrapped tightly around her phone and cheeks more flushed than they were before.

And... are those *tears* in her eyes?

Who do I need to find and kill?

No one makes my wife cry.

I set the smoothies down and walk over to her, resting my hand on her arm to draw her focus to me.

"Hey, what's wrong?"

She tosses her phone on the counter and shakes her head. "My mother is what's wrong."

"What happened?"

She sniffs, a look of resolve appearing on her face, like the last thing she wants is to let her mother bring her to tears.

"I called last night to tell her we got married. She didn't answer, so I just said I had exciting news. When I told her, she seemed happy—if surprised—then asked about you. All I had to do was say a few words, and she figured out who you were. She found your social media and a picture of us and proceeded to critique every little thing about it."

She sighs, shutting her eyes for a moment and taking deep breaths, but when she opens them again, her eyes are glassy.

"She said I should've smiled better, done my hair differently, and if I was planning on getting married, I should've told her so she could've found a diet for me." She clears her throat and looks away. "She said I looked out of place next to you. And though she didn't outright say it, her tone conveyed what she meant by that. I looked like a girl in a frumpy garbage bag compared to the glowing, handsome man next to me."

Rage burns in my gut, but I tamp it down and focus on Jade. She doesn't need my rage. She needs my comfort.

Cupping her face in my hands, I turn her head until her eyes land on mine again.

"Fuck her."

"Justin—"

"No. I mean that. Every letter of every word. And if she ever says shit like that in front of me—if I ever overhear you on the phone and suspect that's what she's saying—I won't be nice. I'll morph into the biggest asshole you've ever met and tell her precisely what I think of her and where she can go."

Because fuck anyone who treats people the way Jade's mom is treating her. Her own daughter.

Jade laughs, but it's more in defeat.

"Darlin', I'm going to need you to listen when I say this. You are beautiful in every possible way. You don't need a diet, a different hairstyle, some other smile, or another dress. You are perfect as you are. And in our wedding photos, you are the shining star. Everything else pales in comparison to you, so do not for a second let her unkind words get in your head. They aren't true, and you deserve better than that. Better than her."

I sweep my thumbs over her cheeks as she stares up at me.

"Justin," she breathes, all the pain gone from her eyes as desire blooms in them.

"You have no idea what you do to me."

I pull her closer, then spin her around, leaning her against the kitchen island. My hand slips to the back of her neck as she licks her lips, chest rising and falling with heavy breaths.

God, I need her. Need her lips on mine. Need to know what it feels like to have her curves pressed against me. What it would be like to be buried inside her.

I fight back a whimper as I lower my mouth to hers, giving her time to stop me. But she doesn't. She leans in, ready for me.

Her breath tickles my lips, and—

Clunk.

Thunk.

We jolt back at the loud noises, followed by some soft metal whirring and a final clank.

What the fuck?

CHAPTER SIXTEEN

Jade

MY FUCKING air conditioner just cock blocked me.

One of the selling points of this place was the central air for both apartments. What no one mentioned was that the damn thing breaks down regularly. It passed all the tests the home inspector did, but a week after moving in three years ago, it broke down. It broke down one other time that summer, and since then, it breaks down multiple times each summer.

It's always some little fix. I half wonder if they're using disposable parts when they fix these things, but I'm desperate for AC, so I don't question anything.

The second summer I lived here, I put a small unit in my bedroom window and paid for one for the unit below me as well. I can work out of my bedroom, eat my meals in my bedroom, and generally survive in my bedroom. Most importantly, I can be cold while I sleep. If I'm not, I don't sleep at all.

"What was that?" Justin asks.

"The bane of my existence," I groan. Off his confused look, I continue. "The air conditioner just went out."

"Does that happen a lot?"

"Only during the summer."

He gives me a flat look, then realization hits. "That's why you have an air conditioner in your room too."

"Yep. I'll call the repair place."

He waves a hand, then plucks their card off the fridge. "I've got it. Take your smoothie and go get your AC running, so you won't be overheated. I can make the call."

"Are you sure?"

He leans in and kisses my forehead. "Let your husband handle this."

I stare at him for a beat. "I suppose I can let you be the man of the house."

He nods toward the hallway. "Go on."

"Thanks."

"No problem."

He stares at me until I finally leave the room, and I have to admit, there's something nice about having someone else to help handle all the little things.

I CAN'T STOP THINKING about Justin. We ordered takeout for dinner so we wouldn't have to heat the kitchen, then we sat on the back porch for a bit, relaxing, since there was a nice breeze. It's obvious he's more equipped than I am to handle the heat, but all I can think right now is that he's out in the stupidly hot living room, while I'm in here enjoying all the cool air.

He's used to it, I tell myself.

He grew up in Georgia.

Maybe he likes sleeping warm.

Or maybe he's on the couch tossing and turning and can't sleep at all.

It should only be one night because they're coming to fix it tomorrow. I have a pre-op appointment, then need to go get some easy to put on clothes and a few other things I need before my surgery on Friday. Justin jumped in and said I still need to do all that, and he'd wait here all day.

I look at the empty space next to me and close my eyes.

I'm the worst wife ever.

Forcing my eyes open again, I throw the covers off and climb out of bed, telling myself I'm doing this for the right reasons—so my husband won't melt—and not the wrong ones. Like wondering what it would be like to sleep next to him. Or cuddle with him. Or—*nope.* Not going there.

When I walk out to the living room, Justin is lying on his back on the couch, no blankets on, an arm tossed over his face, and chest glistening with sweat.

"Justin," I loudly whisper, trying not to wake him up too aggressively.

He jolts awake. "Huh? What's going on?" He blinks at me a couple of times, then lurches forward. "Are you okay?"

He's sleeping out here overheated, and he's worried about me?

"Are you? You look like you're sweating to death."

He looks down, then waves a hand. "I'm fine."

"No, you're not."

"Jade—"

"Come on."

His brows dart up. "What?"

"Come on. Come sleep in my room."

He looks at me like he's not sure he should. Then that annoying charming smirk appears. "I knew we'd end up sharing a bed eventually, but I didn't think it would be this soon."

I pin him with a look. A sassy one that makes his smile grow. "I'm sorry I don't want my husband to melt into a puddle. Especially since we just got married. They'd probably accuse me of murder."

He laughs as he climbs off the couch, then grabs my arm, looking at me sincerely. "You don't have to."

"I want to. My bed is huge. My room is cold. Come get some decent sleep instead of sweating all night."

He stares at me for a beat longer. "If you're sure."

"I'm sure. And don't worry. I don't bite. Unless you ask me to." I give him a flirtatious smile to put him at ease, then head back down the hall.

When we get to my room, he pauses inside the doorway and lets out a long breath of relief. "Thank you."

"No problem."

"Do you have a side of the bed you prefer?"

I shake my head. "I usually end up in the middle, but most of my stuff is in the nightstand on the right, so you can take the left side."

"Got it."

We stare at each other for a long moment, then he gestures to the bed as if I've forgotten what we're supposed to be doing.

I didn't forget. I'm a little distracted. Because it's suddenly dawning on me he's only wearing sleep shorts, and I'm wearing a loose tee with boy short undies. And we're going to sleep next to each other all night.

I can't breathe.

But when Justin raises his eyebrows, I give him a smile that hopefully doesn't make me look psychotic and climb into bed. Lying flat on my back with my arms at my sides.

This is fine.

"Thank you," Justin says again.

"No problem."

"Well, uh, goodnight."

"Night," I chirp.

I swear I hear a stifled laugh, but I close my eyes tight, breathe deep, and try to drift off without moving an inch.

JUSTIN HAS A BIG COCK.

And it's... staring at me.

I lift the sheets again and look down at it, all hard and right there.

Oh god, I'm a perv.

If a guy in one of my romance books did this, it would not be okay.

Although you typically can't see a girl being turned on. But creepily staring wouldn't be okay.

Consent is a thing.

That's it.

I'm about to push the covers off and covertly roll out of bed when Justin stirs.

What do I do?

Look at the ceiling? Pretend to be asleep? Act casual, like there isn't a tent over his crotch that a whole ass group of Boy Scouts could camp under?

Thankfully, he rolls away from me.

I slowly exhale, trying to keep it from being audible, then dramatically yawn and stretch.

Justin inhales deeply, then looks over his shoulder at me. "Mornin'."

"Morning." And my voice is an octave too high. Great.

"How'd you sleep?"

That dissipates the awkwardness for a moment. "Good. How about you?"

"Also good. Much better than if I'd been tossing and turning on the couch all night."

"Good. I'm glad." I'm calmer now, but my voice is still coming out breathy.

He's still right there.

With his probably-still-hard cock.

And he smells good.

I'm not okay. Send help. Or a vibrator. A Justin-free space where I can use my vibrator.

"Okay if I go shower?" he asks.

I glance at him. Did the universe hear my plea?

"Yeah, of course. I'm just going to... lounge for a bit. Maybe get a little work in before I have to leave."

He nods. "Thanks."

Then he's climbing out of bed, and though I shouldn't look, I can't tear my eyes away, wondering if I can get another glimpse of him, but he keeps his body angled away from me. On purpose?

The second the lock on the bathroom door clicks, I dive for my bedside table and pull out my favorite vibrator. It's quiet, but powerful. Exactly what I need to get the job done.

The shower turns on, and I breathe out a sigh of relief and switch my vibrator on. The second it touches my clit, I'm fighting back my moans. I'm too keyed up. I need the release.

My mind drifts back to what I saw this morning, then I imagine his hand around that hard muscle as he holds it in front of my mouth. I close my eyes and imagine swirling my tongue over his tip and the guttural moan he'd make.

I bite my lip, but can't hold back a whimper.

My fingers clench the sheets. I'm so close.

Then my mouth falls open as I imagine taking him deep, choking on him—*fuck.*

Whiny moans slip out of me as my orgasm ripples through me, first in soft waves and then hard pulses.

I go limp against the bed, heart pounding.

Of all the things I thought might be difficult about living with Justin, how horny I'd be for him didn't even cross my mind. If the tension keeps running this high, I'll be lucky to survive the week without spontaneously combusting—or spontaneously orgasming—in front of him.

CHAPTER SEVENTEEN

Justin

HOLY FUCK.

I am not okay.

Not at all okay.

I just saw Jade come.

I didn't intend to see it. But I heard a weird noise coming from her bedroom and I wanted to be sure she was okay. That noise was her making the most sinful moans as she came. As much as I would've loved to have watched all day, I quickly shut the door.

I dip my head under the shower, which should probably be ice cold at this point, but I'm shameless as I wrap my hand around my cock.

It was bad enough to know she was watching me and my morning wood. Her shifting in bed is what woke me up, and why I rolled over. I could sense she was getting jittery. Part of me wanted to roll the opposite direction, though. To roll on top of her, pin her to the bed, and thrust inside her. To swallow those sweet moans and keep them for myself. To watch her beautiful face go slack as she came undone.

Fuck.

I groan as my cum paints the shower wall.

That might be a record for the fastest I've come since I was sixteen.

Bracing my hand on the wall in front of me, I take a deep breath. Living with her might kill me. No. Fighting the tension between us is what's going to kill me. I want to snap, pin her to the wall, and make it clear she's mine.

Not because of a piece of paper.

Because I'm obsessed with everything about Jade Jackson, and there's no doubt she's my person. The one. When you know, you know. Well, I've never been more certain about anything.

She might not be ready to acknowledge it yet, but it won't be long until she's mine in every way.

When Devon and Kennedy were being idiots about their feelings while sharing a damn bed, I told him if you share a bed, sooner or later, you're going to fuck.

Well, if you marry someone out of convenience, then move in together and share each other's space... eventually you're going to fall in love.

It's science.

Or romance.

All I know is I'm falling for this girl, and there's no stopping it, even if I wanted to.

After a quick shower, I dry off and get dressed, thankful I remembered to grab clothes from the living room first.

Or maybe not. I'm wired from all the chemistry sizzling between us, and I want to play. Push some buttons. See where we'll go next.

I left my phone in the bedroom, so I have the perfect excuse to go back in and see what she's doing now. Still, I open the door slowly. I'm not trying to catch her in an intimate moment.

Even if the one I saw earlier will live rent-free in my mind forever.

She's sitting on the bed, laptop on her lap, hair up in a cute little messy bun, and wearing square black-rimmed glasses. I stop and stare at her for a moment. I didn't know she wore glasses.

"Enjoying the view?" she asks playfully.

Flashing a smile, I stroll over to her. "Didn't know you wore glasses."

Her eyes lift to mine. "Yeah. My eyes aren't too bad, so I can see to walk around and stuff, but any tasks that require precision or focus I need my contacts or glasses. And after several days of nonstop contacts, my eyes need a break."

"I like them. They're giving hot librarian vibes."

She rolls her eyes. "That's such a cliché. It's either librarian or teacher or the not popular girl who takes her glasses off and straightens her hair, then magically becomes super hot."

Leaning down, I brush my finger along her jaw. "Fine. You look studious. Professional. Like a hot as fuck boss babe."

She looks up at me, matching my smirk. "You prefer having a boss babe to take the lead? Or do you like to take things into your own hands?"

I swear her eyes dart to the bathroom door when she says that.

Does she know what I did in there?

Is she asking me?

I lean down, my lips grazing her cheek as I whisper, "I'll take either one."

She lets out a shuddery breath, her eyes locking on mine again as I pull away.

Her hot gaze burns into me as I smile and round the bed, grabbing my phone off the bedside table and heading for the door.

But before I leave, I turn back to her. She's still looking at me. And I can't help myself.

"By the way, wifey, if you ever need any help getting off, feel free to ask your husband."

I watch her just long enough to see her eyes widen in surprise, though it's impossible to miss the desire dancing in them as well.

I'm roasting as I walk out of her room, consumed by the fire building between us. Now I'm hoping Jade will leap into the flames with me.

Metaphorically. Because the air conditioner will be fixed today. Permanently. Hopefully, Jade won't kill me when she finds out why.

CHAPTER EIGHTEEN

Jade

I CAN'T STOP THINKING about Justin.

I am not okay.

By the way, wifey, if you ever need any help getting off, feel free to ask your husband.

I can't believe he actually said those words. Right to my face. With that smolder thing he does with his eyes.

"Your blood pressure is a little elevated today. Are you feeling okay?"

My eyes dart to the nurse. Whoops. Probably shouldn't be getting all hot and bothered while she's taking my blood pressure.

"Is it high?"

"Higher than your normal, but still in the optimal range."

I let out a breath, then put on a smile. "I'm a little stressed. Our air conditioner broke yesterday, and I'm hoping the repair person can get it fixed today. I don't do well with heat."

She waves a hand. "Say no more. That would stress me out too."

Crisis averted.

She goes through a bunch of questions and some preparation information with me, and even though I want to ask a thousand questions about the recovery process, those are better saved for my doctor.

"Now, you obviously won't be able to drive after you have the procedure done. Will you have someone with you who can drive you? Or someone who can pick you up?"

"My husband will be here."

She frowns and looks back at the screen. "We have you listed as unmarried here."

"Oh, uh, it's new. Last weekend. We were in Las Vegas and had a whirlwind wedding."

The nurse beams at me. "Good for you. Life's too short not to live a little."

I chuckle at that. If only she knew how much I was *living* right now. Self-publishing was the greatest risk I ever took until now. But the scarier thing is that marrying Justin never felt like a risk. I'm not sure if that's a red flag or a green one, but so far, this man has been throwing up all the green flags, and I'm ready to hit the gas and *go*.

We haven't even kissed since our wedding—though we came close yesterday—but I want more. Not only more kissing. More of him. And physically... I want everything.

A small voice in the back of my mind whispers the words I'm afraid to admit.

I want everything else with him too.

THE RELIEF I felt at walking into an air-conditioned apartment this afternoon was instantaneous. Even though Justin spent the day insisting everything was going fine, I was still worried.

I did my best to not be too annoying with my need for updates.

Justin insisted I take my time today and get every little thing done, stop for lunch, grab a coffee, and pick out a good book.

Bewitched Books and Coffee is one of my favorite places on earth. The staff are incredible, they have a great selection of indie authors, they're incredibly supportive of local authors and artists, and they make the best coffee.

I wandered there for quite a while sipping on a latte.

After I got home and took a shower, Justin had dinner waiting.

He never stops. And even though it's a little strange and I'm afraid to get too used to it... I love it. I'm so used to doing everything alone. It's nice not to have to... even if it's something I have to get used to.

After multiple texts this morning asking how things were going, he told me to stop.

Let your husband handle it.

My body flushes at the thought of all the things I'd like him to handle.

The way I'd like him to handle me.

His fingers biting into my hips as he holds me while I ride him.

And now I'm overheated.

Good thing I have a working air conditioner to cool things down.

I stand up and round the couch, heading for the hallway.

"Where are you going?" Justin asks.

"Just turning the AC down."

"I can do it."

He scrambles to his feet and jogs toward me, only to come to a stop next to me as I stare at the thermostat.

A different thermostat.

It's similar to my old one, which must be why I didn't notice it when I walked by earlier, but this is new.

"Why is it different?"

The old one wasn't broken. The only reason I'd need a new one is if they upgraded the system.

My eyes flit to Justin, then I spin on my heel and hurry out the door as Justin calls after me. When I get to the edge of the porch, I look down and see a brand-new air-conditioning unit.

What the hell?

I turn around and almost collide with Justin.

"What did you do?"

"Jade."

"What did you do?"

"Let's talk inside."

"Great plan."

I storm ahead, pissed off.

Because what the hell? They said they were going to repair the damn thing, not put in a whole new unit.

Except they never said that. Because I didn't talk to them.

I'm standing at the edge of the hallway, emotions going through me rapid fire. As much as I can appreciate this, it's a lot.

Everything he's done for me has been a whole freaking lot.

Justin appears in front of me, an easy smile on his face, and he's so damn gorgeous I can't think straight for a second.

So I lean into my frustration instead and pin him with my fiercest glare. "Is that a new air conditioner?"

He rubs his jaw. "You know, I wasn't watching them the whole time. I'll have to go look."

I throw my hands up. "Justin!"

The feral grin that spreads over his face sends a spark of heat through my core.

But no. *No.* Not right now.

"I love when you say my name like that."

"Like I'm going to cause you bodily harm?"

He shrugs. "I know you won't. And that tone is a turn-on."

I take a slow, controlled inhale, then let it all out.

"What did you do?"

He gestures to himself. "I didn't do anything. The nice men from the HVAC company put in a shiny new air conditioner."

Hands on my hips, I move toward him. "And who paid for it?"

"Jade—"

"No. Why did you do that? It was fixable. Why didn't you let them fix it?"

"Because you should have a working air conditioner."

"And I would have!"

He throws an arm out. "For how long? A few weeks until it breaks again?"

"Then I'd have gotten it fixed again. You can't just come in here, throwing your money around. You're already doing too much for me as it is."

Frustrated, I walk past him down the hall to my bedroom. I hate feeling like I owe him. Him doing this makes it feel even more contractual—even though I still don't understand what he's getting out of it.

"Who says it was only for you? I live here too," he says from behind me.

Those words make my burning anger turn ice cold.

I hadn't even considered that he did this for him. Am I that self-centered? Glancing at my bed, my heart aches.

Why would he want to be forced to share a bed with me? Despite all the jokes—

"Jade."

He spins me to face him, as I try to hide the hurt that's over-powering me. Intensity grows in those blue eyes as he stares at me.

Then his eyes go over my shoulder to the bed, and his face falls a little. "That's not what I meant. I only said I did it for me because I'll benefit too. No one likes being overheated, and on the second floor, it would be that way for most of the day. But if it was just me, I'd figure it out. I wouldn't care that much. You're upset I did this, so I was trying to downplay it, but I can't. I did this because *you* deserve to be comfortable in your home and to have less to worry about over the next few months while you're recovering from surgery. I want to give you that peace of mind. I want to take care of you." His voice drops to a hoarse whisper, and his fingers brush my temple as he sweeps some hair behind my ear. "Let me take care of you."

My eyes are locked on his, my hurt and anger both gone. All that's left is warmth. Desire. Desperation for him.

"Then take care of me," I breathe.

He searches my face, lifting my chin.

"What do you mean?" he croaks.

"You told me to ask my husband if I need any help. Well, I need some help. And I want you to take care of all my *needs*."

He crashes into me, arms wrapping around me as his mouth slants over mine possessively.

I've written a lot of book boyfriends, but I've never had someone kiss me like they kiss their women. Sometimes I wondered if it was mostly fiction. But now, Justin is kissing me so... voraciously. Like it would physically hurt him to hold back.

I didn't think I'd be the girl who would want to be owned, but now I know that feeling isn't toxic. It's not about control. It's about giving in to each other, getting lost in each other, and knowing how deeply wanted I am. It's vibrant, wild passion.

He walks me backward toward the bed, and when the backs of my legs hit the mattress, he stops and pulls away, breathing heavily as he looks down at me.

"You take my breath away, darlin'."

I flush at his words. I'm not even naked yet.

Though I don't like the ugly words that dance through my mind, I can't completely tune them out.

What if he doesn't like how I look naked?

"What are you worrying about?"

"It's been a while since I've been naked with someone."

His eyes light up. "Then I feel even luckier. Like all this"—he drags his finger across my collarbone—"has been saved only for me."

I let out a shaky breath. "Just... be gentle..."

He stares at me for a second as what I'm saying clicks. I'm not talking about sex, but how he looks at me. What he says.

"Darlin', if you think there's an inch of your body I won't adore, you're crazy."

Without giving me another chance to think, he pulls my shirt over my head and drops it to the ground.

He bites his lip as he takes me in. "God, baby. You're killing me. So fucking gorgeous."

All the negative thoughts fall away, and I imagine my body naked beneath his. In that image, all I find is beauty. How beautiful my body splayed out for him would be.

He reaches for the button of my shorts, but I stop him with a hand to his chest. "Don't I get to see the abs?"

He laughs and whips his shirt off, wiggling his pecs as he does.

He shudders when I run my hands down his chest, then he's leaning in, lips pressed into the skin of my neck as his fingers curl in my hair.

A rough, agonized moan slips out of him, and I gasp in response.

I've never felt more needed.

He reaches for my shorts again, and this time, I don't stop him.

"I can't wait to feel every perfect inch of you. I... you're so beautiful it's hard to breathe. You are mine, and I am shamelessly obsessed with you. I can't wait to see what your sinful body can do. I can't wait to touch every delicious curve, to taste, tease, and torture you."

"I want all of that," I breathe, overwhelmed by his words. Him calling me his. How tortured his voice was. I never want to stop feeling like the object of his desire.

"Get on the bed," he orders, slipping out of his shorts. "Right in the center. I want you splayed out and waiting for me."

My core throbs at his words. I need him to touch me. Give me *something*.

He stands at the end of the bed, his dick at full mast in his boxers. His eyes roam over me, and he licks his lips hungrily.

I'll do anything to be his next meal.

He climbs over the top of me, then easily removes my bra, groaning in delight at the sight of my breasts.

He firmly grabs one, bringing his mouth to it, sucking and biting at my nipple.

I arch into him, dragging my fingers down his back.

He roughly switches to my other breast before sitting back on his heels.

His smile turns feral as his eyes trail down my body, finding the lacy hipster underwear that can't hide how turned on I am.

"Look at you," he rumbles, dragging his finger over the wet fabric. "So needy." His eyes find mine again. "Tell me what you want."

My mind goes blank. I don't think anyone has ever asked me that before. I must've really dated—and even hooked up with—some duds.

"I don't—uh—I'm a little—"

"What's the matter, my sweet little romance author? I've read the filthy, filthy words you've written. Can't you say them to me?"

"I don't have much real-world experience. I've had hook ups and dated here and there, but never anyone who's explicitly asked what I've wanted. We've always just done things. I voiced what I liked in the moment, but that's all. And it's always been very vanilla."

"Mm. Looks like I've got something to add to the contract."

Confusion ripples through me. "What?"

"Husband will help wife explore and unlock all her sexual desires. As for tonight... you can tell me what you want or let me take the lead until you find your voice."

I'll do anything to be his next meal.

A flash of embarrassment hits as I think about saying the words aloud. Writing them in a fictional manner is entirely different.

"You keep thinking. I'll start with this."

His lips land just above my ankle, and it takes me a second to realize what he's doing. He's kissing me everywhere. As his lips trail up my leg, he skims his finger up my inner thigh, and my core clenches. I'm fraught with desperation.

When he gets to the top of my thigh, he strokes his finger up my center.

"There," I whine. "That's what I want. Lick my pussy. Please."

CHAPTER NINETEEN

Justin

I'VE DIED and gone to heaven.

I'm lying between Jade's legs, her scent teasing me with every inhale as she begs me to eat her pussy.

I could cry with happiness. She is everything I could ever want and so much more.

From the time I was a teenager, I've been obsessed with women and their beautiful bodies. Any shape. Any size. I wanted them all. But Jade is a new level.

I'm unhinged when it comes to her, and the only word that keeps rumbling through my mind is *mine*. She's mine. I've touched her, kissed her, and I'm about to make her come like no one else ever has.

Anyone else tries to touch her, and I'll break their hands.

I'm not a dark romance boy. I'm a good old boy who wants to worship his girl. But even I can't deny how deeply possessive I feel and how animalistic it makes me.

"Justin, please."

"Don't worry, darlin'. I'll take care of you."

Wrapping my hands around her thighs, I lift them over my shoulders, giving me plenty of room to get lost in her. I'm going to savor every moment, every taste, every cry, every scream. I need it all.

Slowly, I pull her to me until her glistening pink pussy is right in front of me. I swirl my tongue around her entrance, groaning the second I taste her sweet and salty flavor. I lap my tongue there for a moment as she whines in desperation. My smile is wicked as I finally let my tongue trail up and swirl around her clit.

Her loud moan reverberates around the room, and it spurs me on. I was having fun teasing her, but I'm barely keeping it together. The friction of the mattress against my cock does little to settle me down, and the desperation in her moans makes me wild.

Gripping her thighs tighter, I eat her pussy like it's the last meal I'll ever eat. Ever need.

"Oh. Fuck. Justin. Yes."

My name on her lips like that is enough to end me.

I need more. Need to feel her beautiful body come.

Her fingers card through my hair, and she grabs on, holding me right where she wants me as she rides my face. I suck on her clit, and she pulls me tighter against her.

"Right there. Please, please."

My only job right now is to make sure she has the best orgasm of her life. I want her to forget anyone else ever existed. It's just me. Us.

Her legs tremble and she cries out, pulling harder on my hair. I flick at her clit with my tongue, and her body goes taut.

"Yes," she cries, and I lift my gaze, watching the way she lights up, her body shaking as her orgasm tears through her.

I keep sucking and licking at her clit until her hands go slack on my head and she pushes me away. But I don't go far, dropping down, I swirl my tongue around her entrance, lapping up every drop as she comes down from her high.

As I sit back on my heels, she slowly pushes upright, eyes locked on me.

Then heat fills her eyes again, and she smiles a wicked, predatory smile.

"Stand up."

I stare at her for a beat, then do as she asked, watching as she slides off the bed too.

"Come this way." She pulls me a few feet from the bed. "Perfect. I need to be able to see your legs tremble while you try to hold off your orgasm."

Jesus fuck.

She drops to her knees in front of me, and with one swirl of her tongue over my tip, my hand is twisted in her hair.

Then she opens her mouth wide and dives forward, taking more than half my cock in her mouth at once.

"Fuck," I growl.

It feels incredible, but that doesn't compare to how she looks, naked, on her knees for me.

With a big inhale, she takes me deep, gagging a little before pulling back. Her hand wraps around the base of my cock, and she lightly strokes me as she teases her tongue around my tip and squeezes my balls.

"Jade." Her name is a desperate groan. No one has ever made me feel like this—made me feel this much.

I want to come down her throat. Come on her perfect tits. Fill her pussy. Claim her as mine in every way.

My abs tighten, and I look down at my trembling legs, and the tantalizing look in Jade's eyes tells me she noticed too.

A shudder rolls up my spine.

Teeth clenched, I mutter, "I'm close."

She changes her position. Keeping one hand on my base and the other on my balls, she bobs up and down on my cock.

Every muscle tightens, and I'm dripping with sweat, shaking with need.

"I'm gonna come, darlin'. Pull off if you don't want—"

She takes me deeper, and I grab her hair tighter, holding her in place as I fill her mouth with my cum.

When she pulls off me, breathing heavily, her hair is a mess and there's cum dribbling down her chin. She's never looked sexier.

My legs are mostly numb, and I can barely stand, but I offer her my hand to help her up.

Pulling her close, so our bodies are flush, I cup her cheek and capture her lips in a deep, raw kiss.

Her tongue twists with mine, and I'm completely lost to her.

We fall onto the bed and slip under the covers, holding each other and kissing like we're the only people in the world and nothing else matters.

I don't know what's going to happen next, but I know I'm never going to be the same again.

I'm hers now, and there's no going back.

CHAPTER TWENTY

Jade

THE GOLDEN HUE of the July morning wakes me out of a cozy sleep. The kind where I barely rustled all night and all my dreams were happy.

As my eyes flutter open, my heart warms at the happy thing that wasn't a dream.

Justin.

I'm nestled against him, and his arm is draped over my waist. A big difference from yesterday morning.

My heart races, remembering how he perfectly owned my body last night. I've never come so hard or so easily from another person before. It's like he knew exactly what I needed, and slowly stoked the fire, getting me there without rushing or forcing anything.

Then those sinful moans he made when I was going down on him? I could've listened to those noises all night. Though sleeping in his arms is... better. More.

Cooking and watching our favorite shows together helps get to know each other better and develop the roots of our friendship.

Sexual stuff is sexual stuff.

But this is bigger. *This* is a marriage. Or a relationship. *Feelings*. And while that's scary because I don't know what it means, I'm really enjoying it.

Justin yawns as he stirs, waking slowly. When his eyes land on me, he smiles contentedly.

"Morning darlin'."

"Morning. Sleep well?"

He stretches and sits up, so I sit up too.

"Great, actually."

"Me too."

We stare at each other for a moment, and I bite my lip.

"Breakfast?" he asks.

As much as I want to beg him to stay in bed with me all day, I chicken out.

"Yeah, sounds great."

He pops a kiss on my cheek and hops out of bed.

The second the bathroom door is closed behind him, I flop against the mattress and run my hands over my face.

Last night was incredible. Waking up in his arms this morning was perfect. I want more.

I look down at the ring on my finger.

Will I have to give it back when this is all done?

Like I'll have to give him up?

For the briefest of seconds, I allow that thought to wreck me, then I force myself out of this bed and out of this mindset.

As much as I'm enjoying this, I need to remember that I don't get to keep it.

MY HEARTBEAT TICKS UP as Justin reaches for the controller to switch off the TV.

The AC is working now.

We got our little sassy fight and subsequent orgasms out.

There's no reason to have him in my bed.

Besides wanting him there.

For now, Jade. For now. For now. For now.

Maybe if I say it enough, it'll get through my thick skull.

Justin stands and stretches, yawning.

I stand too.

Awkwardly.

What am I doing?

What do I want?

What do I dare to risk?

I clear my throat.

"Need any extra blankets? Now that the AC is working again?" I laugh in the most ridiculous high-pitched way.

An amused smile forms on his lips, and he shakes his head.

"Okay then. Uh... goodnight."

He lets out a little chuckle. "Night, Jade."

Forcing out a breath, I spin and hurry out of the room to my bedroom.

I am ridiculous.

I ROLL VIOLENTLY in my bed for the millionth time tonight.

I'm never going to be able to sleep.

Because I'm an idiot who overthinks things.

And worries about things.

Which is why I'm awake at midnight, mind going over every little thing. I want Justin in here with me. I want to feel him wrapped around me. My surgery is tomorrow, and my stress levels are off the charts.

He makes it better.

That's it. I'm pathetic. Pathetically hung up on my fake husband, who I have very real chemistry with. And maybe feelings for.

Ugh. Ugh. Ugh.

But all the *ughs* in the world don't stop me from getting out of bed and traipsing out to the living room.

Justin is sleeping peacefully on the couch, and I almost second-guess my decision, but knowing how nervous I am about tomorrow and how much Justin has infiltrated my brain, I won't sleep at all tonight if I don't do it.

Reaching over the back of the couch, I gently shake his arm. "Justin."

He jolts awake and squints at me. "Jade? Did the air conditioner break? I swear, I'll—"

"No. It's not that." I look back at the hallway, then run my hand through my hair as a blush creeps onto my cheeks. "Nevermind. It's stupid."

He grabs my hand as I go to spin around. "It's not stupid. What's wrong?"

"I can't sleep."

"Why not?"

Before I can say anything, his face morphs into a wicked smile. "Did you get used to having me in your bed?"

I stare at the stupid smirk on his face, warring with myself about what to say.

Tell him what you really want.

I clear my throat. "I'm worried about tomorrow. I could... use a distraction."

Missed it by that much.

For a moment, the playfulness slips off his face. Only a gentle —almost sad—smile appears. But it's gone as quickly as it came, and a troublemaking gleam dances in his eyes.

He's off the couch in a second, prowling over to me. "I'm happy to distract you, wifey." Leaning in, his lips brush my ear. "I'll distract you all night."

Then he's dragging me down the hall to my room and stripping me naked as desire wells inside me.

I can't deny I love this.

Love having his attention on me. Love what his touch does to me. It's too much and not enough all at once.

We crawl under the covers together, kissing as our hands roam.

His fingers dance between my legs as I stroke him, the intensity building until we come together, lips locked and hearts pounding to the same rhythm.

But when my body relaxes and my eyes drift closed, it's not the orgasm but the safety of Justin's arms wrapped around me that lulls me to sleep.

CHAPTER TWENTY-ONE

Justin

I WAKE up to the feeling of Jade's pillowy curves pressed against my body.

This must be what heaven feels like. I could live like this forever.

When she went to bed alone last night, I was kicking myself. I've never slept better than I did with her body tangled with mine. But it felt weird to say, *hey, can I sleep in your bed with you tonight?* It could come off needy or creepy, and those aren't the vibes I'm going for.

But this cozy comfort? I could wake up to this every day and never get tired of it.

Jade rustles, slowly waking up. When she sees me, she smiles happily.

"Hi."

"Morning." Pushing boundaries, I press a kiss to her forehead.

Sure, we kiss during sexual stuff, but we haven't talked about what happens in between, and I'm not sure exactly what she wants.

I know what I want.

Everything.

Hopeless bastard, party of one.

But then she sighs contentedly, and maybe I'm not so hopeless after all.

"What time is it?"

I glance around her at the clock. "Almost seven."

She grimaces and looks at her hand. "I guess it's time to get up and get ready then."

Pushing the covers off, she moves to stand, but I grab her arm. "Hey, wait a minute."

"What?"

"I know you're stressed, so just... come back. Lay here with me for a few more minutes."

She stares at me for a moment, eyes growing sadder until I'm sure she's about to cry. But then she lies back down and rolls to face me. I move closer, wrapping my arms around her.

The ways we've made each other come have been incredible, but they pale in comparison to this. I want more of it. The emotional connection. The snuggles. Yeah, I'm a cuddlewhore, and I make no apologies for it.

The problem is, I don't know what Jade wants. She used orgasms as her reasoning last night, though with how her body is molded to mine now, it seems like she likes this too.

Or maybe she just needs some comfort this morning.

"It's going to be okay," I whisper.

"I know," she says, but I can tell she doesn't really believe it.

That's fine. She doesn't have to. Because I'll be here every step of the way to make sure she's okay.

"KIDDO, you need to take a deep breath or you're going to give yourself a heart attack, and I guarantee you, that's going to be worse to recover from than this surgery," Papa Jackson says from Jade's other side as we sit in the waiting room.

Her procedure will be done while she's awake, and from everything I've read, it should be relatively quick. Recovery looks frustrating, but not terrible. I think Jade has built it up in her head to be worse than it actually will be.

"I'm scared," she whispers.

Running my hand over her back, I wish I could relieve her stress. "I know this is scary for a lot of reasons, but it'll be over before you know it, and we'll be here to make sure you have everything you could possibly need. We're going to get through this together."

Papa Jackson gives me a nod and an approving smile.

"Jade Jackson?" a nurse calls.

"That's me," she squeaks.

I lean in and kiss her cheek. "You've got this. We'll see you soon."

She squeezes my hand and rises from the chair.

"Love you, sweetheart."

She smiles weakly at her dad, then makes her way over to the nurse.

My stomach knots. I hate that she has to go in there alone. I wish I could be with her so I could distract her, make her laugh. Something. Anything.

"She's going to be fine."

I turn to look at her dad, who smiles at me.

"You're almost as much of a basket case as she is. But I like seeing how much you care for my daughter."

"I do," I say genuinely.

He shakes his head and laughs. "I figured that out when you offered to marry her. I'm not an idiot. It was your way of taking care of her and building something with her. Whether she admits it or not, she feels the same way for you. The way she smiled when she was texting you—before you ever met—was unlike anything else. You make her happy and bring out her joyful side. I'm glad she has you, and I'm glad you'll be with her while she recovers. I'd do it in a heartbeat, but she'll be happier with you."

He goes back to reading his magazine like he didn't casually drop all that on me.

I love that he sees it all, and I hope he's right that Jade does too. That she sees me and wants it all.

God knows I want her.

A NURSE ESCORTS me back to the recovery room where Jade is resting, so they can monitor her before she goes home. The nurse said the procedure went well and Jade did great.

When she pushes the door open, Jade's relaxing in a big, comfortable recliner, her arm wrapped up and tucked in a sling. Her eyes pop open, surprise filling them.

The nurse shuts the door behind me, and I walk over to Jade and kiss her forehead.

"Hi."

"Hi. I... wasn't expecting you. They said they were calling someone back. I guess I just assumed it would be my dad."

My heart drops, but I keep a calm face.

"If you want me to go grab him—"

"No. That's not what I meant. I'm glad it's you. Sometimes this still feels like a dream. I'm glad it's not," she breathes. "I like having you here."

"Then this is where I'll be." I drop into the chair beside the recliner and wrap my hand around her good hand. "How are you feeling?"

She sighs, her exhaustion palpable. "Okay. Tired. They gave me some medicine to relax me a little, then numbed me up and did the thing." She grimaces at her hand. "I'm mostly fine now, just hungry and need a nap."

"Your dad brought a cooler of food with him for us to take home. We'll be well fed, and I will make sure you have a nice, comfortable spot to sleep."

"Might have to be on the couch. I'm worried I'll roll too much in bed."

"We can make that work."

She closes her eyes as she leans back against the chair. "Good."

I stroke my thumb over the back of her hand, and she smiles, not opening her eyes.

"I like when you take care of me."

I lift her hand to my lips and kiss it. "Then I always will."

She brushes her thumb over mine, then lets out a long breath. Hopefully, this is a good sign that everything is going to go smoothly.

"YOU NEED TO TAKE THE HYDROCODONE."

Jade sniffs and wipes at her face with her left hand.

Her right hand is perched on a stack of pillows while she sits on the couch.

The doctor said the worst of the pain would be in the first forty-eight hours, and about an hour ago, it hit her. The ibuprofen she took earlier didn't help, and she's been sitting in the corner of the couch, crying for the last half hour. I can't take it anymore. Seeing her cry makes me want to kill someone.

"Baby, I'm worried about you." I kneel in front of her. "Please just take it. If you don't rest, you can't heal."

She didn't want to take any narcotics if she could avoid them, but she needs something to get her through this.

"Okay," she whimpers. "I thought I could handle it."

"Some things aren't meant to be handled alone," I say as I walk to the kitchen.

Finding the prescription, I read the label carefully, then pull out one of the pills and cut it in half before taking it back to her.

"This is the lowest dose. It still might make you a little loopy, but it shouldn't be too bad. And if, for some reason, it doesn't take the edge off, it's perfectly safe to have the other half."

She nods and takes the pill followed by a big glug of water.

Sitting down next to her, I sweep some hair off her face.

"Can you turn your head?"

"That's not what's broken," she says with a pathetic laugh. Then she turns her head toward me.

"Other way."

She squints at me, but does it.

Gently, I run my fingers through her soft hair, then take a few strands in my hand and fumble through braiding them together. I looked up tutorials online, and they seemed easy enough. I figured having her hair out of her face would be a must, and she told me in the past that she didn't like to wear her hair in a ponytail for too long because it hurt after a while.

Painstakingly slowly—and probably really poorly—I French braid her hair.

"What are you doing?"

"Putting your hair back. Just relax." Holding all the strands in one hand, I grab the remote with the other. "Here, put something on."

I get back to braiding, and to my surprise, she doesn't put on *Once Upon a Time*.

"*Virgin River?*"

"Have you ever seen it?" she asks.

"Nope."

I swear she snickers under her breath. "Well, get ready for all the drama. This makes my books look tame."

Somehow, I doubt that's possible, but I'll take her word for it.

After another few minutes, I finish the braid. "Okay, all done."

She turns so her back is against the couch again, then reaches up to feel her hair.

"Thank you," she whispers, then shakes her head. "I can't believe—" Her voice breaks again, and I move closer.

"What?"

"I can't believe you did that for me."

"I'll do whatever you need, darlin'. Now, teach me about this show."

JADE FELL ASLEEP HALFWAY through the first episode. After making sure she was breathing okay, I took a quick shower, grabbed some extra pillows and blankets for the couch, and warmed up some more food.

After eating and watching more of *Virgin River*—which is terrifyingly addicting—I put our bowls in the sink and start making a little bed for myself on the other side of the couch.

"What are you doing?" Jade asks. "Aren't you going to sleep on the couch with me?"

She's loopy from the pain meds and still a little emotional.

"Yeah, that's what I'm doing."

"No. Not there." Emotion swells in her voice again, and I stop and walk over to her. "Will you sleep here? Next to me?"

Oh.

I cup her cheek and sit down next to her as tears spill from her eyes.

"Of course I will. I'll be wherever you want me to be."

I wrap my arm around her shoulders, fingers curling into her messy braid.

"Stay here," she whispers, leaning into me. "Just stay with me."

Her eyes close again, and no matter how loopy she is, I'm still taking her words seriously.

If this is where she wants me to stay, then this is where I'll be. If she wants me by her side, I'll stay here forever.

CHAPTER TWENTY-TWO

Jade

SURGERY CAN SUCK IT.

Why yes, I have lost all ability to form a better sentence than that.

It's been six days since I last wrote. Cue the *It's been eighty-four years* meme, because that's how I'm feeling.

My pain is down significantly since the first couple of days, and I don't need the narcotics anymore. All my memories from the day of my surgery and the following day are a bit hazy. Other than Justin being the absolute sweetest human in existence.

It's killing me a little bit because I don't know if he's a caretaker by nature or if he wants to take care of *me*. Nothing else sexual has happened, and I'm not expecting it to. For once, my horniness has chilled out because everything else about healing has taken precedence.

On the flip side of that, Justin has been sleeping next to me on the couch every night. I'm hoping to move back to my bedroom tonight, and I want him there with me. I sleep better. I'm calmer. I'm happier.

I'm *screwed.*

I want him, and it's so hard to know where we stand with each other or what he wants from me while I'm still healing and need so much help. The last thing I want to do is get into some big conversation about it right now and make things weird. Because I like how he takes care of me.

A few weeks ago, I never would've imagined wanting anyone but my dad to take care of me, but I'm glad it's been Justin by my side. Especially for the sponge bath a couple days in. I was able to do most of it myself, but I still needed his help with a few things. Now I can comfortably sit in the bathtub and wash myself with my left hand. It takes forever, but it's one thing I can do.

I can't wash my hair yet, though. Thankfully, my hairdresser was nice enough to let me come in a couple of days ago, and she washed my hair and styled it. I can get by with dry shampoo for about a week, even if it leaves me feeling a little gross.

I know Justin would wash my hair if I asked, but contorting in the bathtub while he tries to do that sounds uncomfortable at best and dangerous at worst. And I want my hand to heal.

I left myself a long voice note this morning because I had a brilliant idea, but I was still trying to type left-handed or scribble notes along the way, so I didn't forget things I wanted to say later while I was talking.

Being a creator without tools to create is inhumane.

It's cruel and unusual punishment.

So is being stuck on the couch day after day after day.

I don't even know what day it is anymore.

Wednesday? Thursday?

I might be a touch dramatic right now, but I feel good. I want to do things. But my hand is unusable, and it's been pouring rain for two days.

I've got cabin fever *bad.*

I'm losing my mind. My skin is crawling.

And there's a smudge on my glasses that's making my eye twitch, but I haven't been able to coordinate cleaning them effectively one-handed with my non-dominant hand.

Gah!

"What are they doing?" Beside me, Justin throws his hand out at the TV. Then he turns his glare on me. "Why did you do this to me?"

Okay, that gets a smile out of me. Seeing Justin's love-hate obsession with *Virgin River* play out has been fun.

"Glad you're loving it."

He grumbles, but doesn't disagree.

I'm glad he's having fun with it, even if nothing can hold my attention. And I'm tired of the couch. Normally I love my couch, but I've spent all my time there lately. We went for a walk a few days ago, but I swear it hasn't stopped raining since. And I can't get my bandage wet, so here I am.

Cranky.

Meh.

I need... something.

Pushing myself off the couch, I aim for the kitchen, but I'm not really hungry, and nothing sounds good. So, I end up back in the living room. But I don't want to sit down, so I walk through the kitchen again. I do my little roundabout three more times before Justin pauses the TV and stands up.

"Do you need something?"

"Fresh air, the wind on my face."

"Jade..."

"I need to write. I need to do something, anything. But yes, if I could pick one thing, I need to write. I'm going insane. All I want to do is get the words that won't leave me alone out of my head. I want to let them live and breathe and find their story." I start pacing, the anxious energy inside me all spilling out. "And all I keep thinking is, what if, for some reason, this didn't work? Or it gets worse? What if I have to go through this over and over and it never gets better? What if I had to stop writing—"

"You will never have to stop writing. I will find you the best dictation software on the planet. I don't care how expensive it is. Or if you want me to and can trust me with it, I'll help you write. It's different from dictation, and I can learn to type faster. We can figure it out."

"You only care because you want to know what happens in the Marianos series."

That was a bitchy thing to say, and I know it. I shouldn't be taking my crankiness out on him, but... maybe a part of me needs to know that's *not* why he's doing it. I need to know the truth behind his words. If he cares the way he seems to.

He walks over and rests a hand on my cheek, unfazed.

"No, I care because I hate seeing you unhappy. And if I can fix it, I will. If I can't, hopefully I can pay someone who can."

My face crinkles, relief flooding me, and also guilt.

"I'm sorry. You shouldn't have to deal with me like this."

"Like what?"

"Cranky, angry, and incapable of doing basic things by myself."

Now his other hand is on my cheek as he cups my face. "Darlin', I signed up for this. It's what a marriage is. Good, bad, I don't care. I'm here. Let me take care of you."

Stupid tears fill my eyes. Whenever he says stuff like that, it feels real. It makes me long for this to be real. And then I feel guilty again because I'm not giving him nearly as much as he's giving me.

"Stop stressing," he whispers. "Relax. I know there are a lot of things you *want* to do, but let's find something you *can* do."

"Any suggestions?" I ask.

"Actually, yes. I don't know how you'll feel about it, but I think it could be a good use of your time if you're willing to try."

Now I'm just confused.

"Okay..."

"Come with me."

He takes my good hand and leads me down the hall to the

extra room. He's been working on it while I've been recovering, so I haven't seen the setup yet.

When we get inside, he takes me into the large booth he built, and I'm confused when I find two microphones there.

"Why are there two?"

He swallows hard, looking a little uncertain. "I was hoping you'd be willing to try recording with me. I thought we could work on your first interconnected standalone series together. You have a beautiful voice, and while there will still be a learning curve, I think you can do this, and it will give you something to focus on while you can't write."

I stare at him with big eyes. My throat feels tight, and it's hard to swallow.

"You did this for me?"

"For us. Selfishly, I think we could have a lot of fun recording together. I'd love to give it a try. And I can give you some tips and instruction as we go. Worst case, we hate it, but I don't have another narrating job booked until late August, so we have time to play."

"Okay."

His face lights up. "Yeah?"

"Yes."

He jumps into action. "Okay. I have your first interconnected standalone ready to go."

"Wait, how?"

"I got it off your laptop while you were high on the good drugs."

"Sneaky."

He shrugs. "I was excited by the idea."

"Well, keep it together until we see how I do. This could be legitimately terrible."

"Then at least we'll have a good laugh. Come on, darlin'. I'll get you all set up."

THIS IS REALLY FUN. I mean, I have no idea what I'm doing, and I'm constantly getting instruction from Justin and rerecording things, but it's a lot of fun. Bringing my words to life gives me a rush of excitement I haven't had in a long time.

We're recording them duet style, so me speaking the female parts and him speaking the male parts no matter whose POV we're in.

When we played the first chapter back, I found plenty of places where I can improve, but I *loved* it. It also awakens a part of me I haven't used in a long time. My junior and senior years of college, I started doing improv. I'm fairly extroverted, but I tended to struggle with extemporaneous speaking, and it gave me some social anxiety. My dad suggested improv, and I thought he was crazy. Getting on stage and feeling uncomfortable in front of people? But it helped me a lot, and I credit it with my comfort at events and signings, and even my ability to talk with readers and other authors.

Recording with Justin, I'm remembering some of the lessons I learned there.

"What do you think?" Justin asks, removing his headphones.

"This was a brilliant idea. And I'd love to keep going. It might be a labor of love while I learn, but—"

"I don't care. I'm in."

"Thank you for doing this. It's an outlet I didn't know I needed, but it instantly calmed some of the restlessness I've been feeling."

"Good. That's what I was hoping for."

He leans in and kisses my forehead, sending butterflies dancing through my stomach.

"More tomorrow?" I ask.

Justin smiles. "As much as you want."

I wrap my good arm around him in a hug, closing my eyes and breathing deep, inhaling his scent as I revel in the feeling of his body so close to mine. In the peace I feel with his arms around me.

The only words that dance though my brain are *please, let this be real*. Because all I want is more of this. More little moments. More of whatever it is that's blossoming between us. More of us.

DESPITE HOW CRANKY I was earlier, the afternoon recording really turned things around. It also got my creative juices flowing, and after a bath, I sat down and typed a bit with my left hand. It was arduous and didn't last long because I didn't want to cause issues with my left hand too, but it was *something*.

Justin went to shower after I took a bath, but the shower's been off for a bit now, and I'm not sure where he is. Knowing him, he's stealing more books off my computer. Not that I'm complaining. It was incredibly sweet and a lot of fun.

I still feel like I'm taking more than I'm giving in this relationship, but that's just me.

"Well, I didn't ask for your opinion." Justin's sharp voice rings out as he walks down the hall.

I've only ever heard that tone in his voice one other time. When that creep touched my ass in the bar the night we met.

He goes into the kitchen, body laced with tension, as I watch from the couch, unsure what I should do.

"This is exactly why I didn't feel at home there anymore. I don't—no. Frankly, I don't care what you think. My life is my own. Feel free to respect that or get out of it."

He slams his phone down on the counter, and I scramble off the couch and into the kitchen. He's facing away from me, hand in his hair, so I walk over and rub my hand down his back.

He jumps at the touch, but then relaxes into it and slowly spins around. "Sorry."

"For what?" I ask.

He waves toward his phone. "My parents... they just—" He growls. "I'm pissed, but you don't need that."

"Excuse me?" I press my fingers into his cheek, turning his head so I can meet his eyes. "You can be here for me and help me and put up with my shitty attitude, but the second you're a little upset, you apologize to me? Try again. Feel whatever feelings you need to. Better yet, let them out. Talk to me. You said this is what you signed up for, well, newsflash, you didn't coerce me into it. I signed up for it too. Let me help you."

His emotion-drenched eyes lock on mine, and slowly, he nods.

Taking his hand, I lead him over to the couch.

Once he's sitting down, I curl up next to him.

"So, this is one of the *getting to know you* things we skipped over, but I think it's important that we talk about it now. All you've really said is that you're not close with your parents, and it would be toxic if you tried to be."

He looks at me with soft eyes, then wraps his arm around me.

"When I left home for college in Chicago—where I met Devon and Kennedy—my parents made it a point to tell me over and over that I chose to leave our family behind. That was never my intention, but as idyllic and peaceful as our little town seemed, it was also small. I wanted to see the world. For some reason, my parents hated that."

He sighs and runs a hand through his hair.

"I understand why a bit more now. Because when I came home, searching for that same feeling of cozy small-town peace, it was harder to find because I saw the world differently. Maybe it wasn't my town as a whole, but there are a subset of people there who are close-minded and downright hateful at times. Unfortunately, my parents are a part of that."

"Were they always that way?"

He shakes his head. "I don't know. To some degree, at least. From a distance, my relationship with my parents seemed fine. They were always invested in local politics and involved with the church. Though sometimes Mom was a little too involved with everyone else's lives, I didn't think much of it. But when I got home, I saw a different side of them."

He sighs heavily.

"I made an effort to spend time with them, usually with a weekly dinner, but most of them were spent with my mom gossiping about someone in the church. Usually someone who needed love and support, not judgment. Dad wasn't any better, mostly talking down about some group of people or another. My mom was trying to control my life because she didn't agree with most of my choices, and my dad was disgusted that I love romance and narrate romance. He kept flipping between asking if I was gay or suggesting I have a porn addiction."

My brows shoot up. That's horrible. And the absolute worst bullshit stereotype about the genre and people who enjoy it.

"Seeing them be so damn hateful ripped that feeling of home away. I grew to resent them for the way they treated people. The way they treated me. I went to say goodbye to them before the signing, since I knew I might not come back after, and there was an anti-trans sign in their yard. I drove around the block three times before I finally forced myself to park and go in, disgusted by that sign. And when I said something, all I got was a guilt trip about how the city changed me which led to a guilt trip about me leaving again. That phone call tonight was more of the same. When I see the relationship you have with your dad or Devon has with his parents—hell, the relationship *I* have with his parents—it kills me that I couldn't have the same thing."

Leaning up, I kiss his cheek.

"Thank you for telling me. I'm sorry you have to deal with them because you deserve so much better. Just know if you ever want or need to go back there, I'll be right by your side."

He shakes his head.

"That's the last thing I want. I don't want to deal with them, and I have no desire for you to meet them because I'm not proud of them. And frankly, I'm worried they'll be unkind to you. The last thing I ever want to do is put you in a situation to be hurt by anyone."

My heart aches at his words, but for the first time, I understand what he's getting out of this. He might not be able to put it into words, but this is what he's been searching for. What he's wanted. Support. A family. A home.

I'll happily give him all of that.

"You're not alone," I whisper. "You have a beautiful friend group. They love you like a family should. But you also have me. I'm your family now too. And so is my dad. If you want that type of relationship with him, he'll give it to you without a second thought."

He tucks some hair behind my ear, looking at me reverently. "You have a beautiful heart, and you're way too good for me."

I stare up at him. "And I've spent the last week thinking you're giving me more than I'm giving you. We've both been wrong."

His eyes meet mine for another beat, then he softly nods, running his fingers up and down my arm.

I snuggle close and hand him the remote. "It's *Mandalorian* time. I need to know what happens next, and you need to impress me with more random details."

Some of the sadness washes away. "I'd be happy to."

WHEN OUR SHOWS are done for the night, Justin turns off the TV and reaches for the pillows, to start making our bed, but I grab his hand.

"Actually, I was thinking I'd like to sleep in my room tonight."

His brows go up, then a touch of sadness ghosts his eyes.

I clear my throat and force myself to be a little vulnerable. He was so open with me earlier. If he says no, I'm strong enough to handle it.

"Um, would you sleep in there with me?"

His eyes lock on mine.

"Just in case I need... anything," I whisper.

And just like that, the sadness is gone, and his eyes are bright again.

"If that's where you want me, darlin', that's where I'll be."

I let out a shaky breath. "Okay. Good."

While I get ready in the bathroom, Justin heads to my room, and when I walk in, I find the bed all set up with pillows to rest my arm on.

"I know you said your stuff is in the other bedside table, but I figured it was better to have your arm on the outside of the bed rather than the inside."

"That's fine. Thank you."

He goes to get ready while I get settled in bed, and when he returns, he crawls into bed carefully, leaving space between us that feels cold and wrong.

Reaching over, I run my hand down his arm.

"You don't have to be all stiff or keep space between us. No nuns are going to jump out of my closet and hit you with a ruler. We've been cuddled up on the couch all week. I can handle a little more." I mash my lips together. "If you want."

He gazes at me for a moment, then smiles softly and wraps an arm around me.

He doesn't say anything, but I know what he's thinking because it's running through my mind too.

I could get used to this.

CHAPTER TWENTY-THREE

Jade

I'M GETTING USED to this.

For the last nine days, Justin has slept in my bed each night. And each morning, I've woken up with his body curled around mine.

Maybe it's all a mistake. Maybe I'm going to end up with a broken heart.

Or maybe this is all leading us exactly where we're supposed to be.

That's what my romantic heart believes.

And that's what the feelings that are rapidly growing for Justin want to be the truth.

We need to talk about it. I know we do.

Today I get my bandage off. A little over two weeks, and I'll finally be able to do a bit more on my own. And after my first physical therapy session on Friday, hopefully I'll be cleared to start typing again.

And now that Justin and I are getting past the caregiver-patient dynamic, maybe we can figure out what's happening between us.

Get it all out in the open.

Because miscommunication never got anyone anywhere.

But that doesn't mean I'm not stressing and overthinking it and living in fear of this cozy little bubble bursting.

I look over at Justin's sweet, sleepy face, and all I want is this. For him to be mine. For this to be real.

I hope it is.

"THIS IS IT. ARE YOU READY?" the orthopedic physician assistant asks me.

"After two weeks of being wrapped up? Yes, I'm ready for my arm to be free."

Finally!

"Good. Let's get to it."

I've been feeling pretty good for the past week. I haven't had any pain and the swelling has been under control. I'm ready to get this bandage off and work toward getting back to my life. Though recording audio with Justin has kept my mind focused, it's also sparked my creative side, and I'm ready to start typing again.

"I need you to hold still for me," the physician assistant says.

Beside me, Justin stifles a laugh.

"Sorry. I'm a little excited."

"That's fair, but I'd rather not cut you. That'll make the whole process take longer."

"Take a breath, darlin'. You'll be free in no time."

My eyes drift to him and my heart ignites.

That's the usual reaction these days.

It's going to kill me if he doesn't want this too. So I'm trying not to overthink things and believe in what I've seen. The type of love story I've written for years. Maybe not quite that dramatic. Angst is a lot more fun to read about than it is to live.

The PA cuts through the outer layers of the bandage, then unwraps the inner layers, and when my arm is finally free, I sigh in relief. He also snips the stitches on my palm.

"You'll want to moisturize and massage there daily to help keep it from cramping and to minimize scarring."

I nod, then he asks me to move my fingers, and… it's not easy. My range of mobility is very limited, and I can't even make a fist.

"Whoa, that's so weird."

"Is that normal?" Justin asks.

The PA nods. "Yep. Muscle mass decreases quickly when there's minimal use. But that's what PT is for. They'll help regain that strength, and it looks like you'll have some OT for fine motor skills as well. It takes time, but a good chunk of that hand strength will return over the next couple of months, as long as you're working at it."

"Oh, I will be. I've got worlds to dive back into."

The PA looks confused, and Justin jumps in. "She's an author."

"Oh. Well, I'm sure the physical therapist will encourage you to get back to typing sooner than later because it's good for blood flow and strengthening, and it'll help with range of motion, but they'll set guidelines and limits when you see them. Now, for the most important question. Any pain when you move your fingers or your wrist?"

I move them the minimal amount I can, my eyes getting a bit watery when I don't feel any pain.

"No. Nothing."

"Good. The hope is that will continue to be the case and we'll consider you fully healed. Time will tell, but that's the outcome for the majority of people. Follow all the instructions you get and don't overdo things, and I think you'll be fine."

"Thank you so much."

"No problem. Any other questions?"

I shake my head, happiness flooding me. I finally feel like I'm on the upswing. It never really hit home that the whole point of this was to be pain free. I'd had some form of pain for so long, I couldn't conceive what it would be like to not have any. Now this is all starting to feel worth it.

"No. I think I'm good."

He gives me a few more instructions—like still wearing the sling as needed to help keep my hand elevated—then I'm free to go.

As we walk out of the office, Justin takes my hand, and my heart lights at the unlikelihood of it all. A little over a month ago, I left the office in tears, afraid I might lose a piece—if not all—of my career from this. I was with my dad, but beyond him, I felt very alone, especially when it came to managing all this.

Now my husband is by my side and has been through every moment. The way he's cared for me made every step of this process so much easier to deal with.

The husband part might only be legal, but this doesn't feel fake anymore. My heart flutters as it tries to convince me... maybe this never was.

AFTER COFFEE and a little shopping trip to celebrate and get me some better fitting headphones for recording, we're at my dad's house for dinner.

"Papa Jackson, what smells delicious in here?"

"Don't get too excited. It's just a simple casserole. It's called Hungry Jack."

"Oh my gosh. We haven't had that in forever. I need the recipe. It's so good." I look at Justin. "Baked beans and sautéed ground meat and onions with barbecue sauce, then topped with cheddar biscuits. It's delicious."

"I also made a tossed salad with homemade Italian dressing. And I might've made some peanut butter pie."

"With the Oreo crust?" I smile as he nods. "Thanks, Dad."

"Well, we're celebrating. Your arm is free and you're recovering... you look happy, honey."

"That she does," Justin says, his handsome smile twisting up my insides.

My gaze goes from Justin, who is at the fridge getting drinks, to my dad. "I am happy."

Happier than I realized.

God, I hope I get to keep it.

"YOU'RE GOING to let me do the dishes whether you like it or not. I swear, I'll call Michelene and tell on you," Justin says to my dad, referencing his girlfriend, who is having a ladies' night with a few friends tonight.

"You're a dictator," my dad says to Justin, but I just laugh.

"He is very bossy."

My dad's already walking toward the living room when I say that, and Justin spins around from his spot at the sink, lifting a brow and staring at me, gaze heated.

So soft it's barely a whisper, he says, "You like it."

I slowly shake my head, but I can't stop the smile that creeps up my lips.

After doing everything for myself for years—for the most part, at least—it's nice to have someone tell me to sit down instead of doing all the things.

"Are you sure you don't need help?" Because I will never, ever take him for granted.

"No. Go rest. Consider that an order."

I laugh a little. "Yes, sir."

I walk through the swinging door out to the living room and take a seat on the couch opposite my dad's favorite chair, where he's already sitting.

"You really are happy. I swear I could see your smile shining even in the dark."

My cheeks heat a bit, but I can't deny it. I've been smiling a lot more often lately.

"Thanks, Dad."

"Does that mean all this is official between you two now? More official than the piece of paper you signed?"

I sigh at that. "I'm... working on it."

Dad's brow furrows. "Well, stop *working* and do what you need to do."

"You sound like a more crass version of Yoda." Justin's love of *Star Wars* is rubbing off on me.

"No, I just don't want to see this kind of joy and love pass you by."

"Love? Don't get ahead of yourself."

I care for Justin. I have feelings for him. But love...

Love forms in a second, but grows over a lifetime.

Has that love already formed? Is it a seed we've planted?

That's a little too overwhelming to think about right now.

"Don't deny that whatever this is has or could grow into love."

Could.

It probably *will.*

"Is that crazy? Or fast? Too much too soon?"

Dad shakes his head. "Too soon is an excuse people use when they're afraid. Before you even knew him in person, he made you smile like no one ever had. Not the high school boys you were giddy over, not the boyfriends you hesitantly introduced me to, not the non-serious guys you never wanted me to see. With Justin, you light up. I know you're afraid because it happened fast or not the way you intended. I also know when you're in the middle of it, sometimes it's hard to see objectively. Here's some objectivity. That man cares for you the way I could only dream someone would care for my daughter. It's obvious in everything he does. There's no stamp of approval harder to earn than mine, and he's got it. Stop overthinking things. Don't let your fears or uncertainties get in the way. You're stronger and smarter than that. Besides, you wouldn't be who or where you are today if you let fear hold you back. Live the life you deserve. Don't ever hold yourself back."

I glance toward the kitchen.

Justin needs to wash the dishes faster because I'm ready to get him home so we can talk.

Home.

When he suggested us living together, that felt as crazy as getting married, but now I couldn't imagine being there without him.

It's not only my home anymore, it's his too. I need to make sure he knows that. And that a house isn't the only thing that's his. I am too, and I have been for a while now.

DON'T OVERTHINK.

I've been chanting it the whole way home, but the closer we get, the more my mind races. I need to talk to him. Lay it all out.

I'm practically buzzing when he finally pulls into the driveway, and I throw my door open a little too forcefully, but this is eating away at me. I have to know. Have to face it all head-on.

I want it to be real.

The signs say yes, but what if I'm misreading them?

I've written a lot of romance, but my real-life experience is limited. Mostly because I was looking for that book boyfriend guy. And after a few months when none of my actual boyfriends came close to that, I dumped them.

I started to wonder if maybe the book boyfriend I was looking for was truly a work of fiction. But Justin is a living, breathing embodiment of one.

The question is... is he mine?

"Are you okay?" Justin asks once we've made it through the door of the apartment.

I spin to look at him, shaking with nervous energy and anticipation.

"Um, yes..."

"That sounded more like a question. What's going on?"

My eyes dart around. I don't want to have this conversation in the entryway.

I gesture toward the hallway.

"Come with me."

We end up standing just inside my bedroom, staring at each other.

"Darlin', what's wrong?"

My eyes slip closed, emotion rustling through me. "It kills me when you call me that."

His hand skims my cheek and my eyes flash open.

"Why?"

"Because I never want you to call anyone but me that ever again."

He bites his lip, then smiles. "Want me to put it in the contract?"

"Fuck the contract."

His brows shoot up. "What?"

"That was for a fake marriage, but now... maybe the marriage part is only legal, but there's something real between us. Right?" My cheeks heat, but I don't break our gaze.

A smile of pure happiness grows on his face as joy shimmers in his eyes.

"Darlin', why do you sound like you're questioning that?

This thing between us has never been fake. There's nothing more real than my feelings for you."

I inhale sharply at that. Those words are more than I hoped for.

"You've been mine since the night we met, and you've been burrowing into my heart since we first started talking. We're writing our love story, and it's the last one you're going to have, so stop worrying and start enjoying it."

I throw my arms around him and lean into him, slanting my mouth over his.

A low groan sounds in his throat as he wraps his arms around me and deepens our kiss, his tongue sweeping into my mouth.

He walks me backward to the edge of the bed, then lifts his lips from mine, breathing heavily.

"I need you to know something," I whisper. "Every night I asked you to sleep in my bed, it wasn't for any of the reasons I said. It was because I wanted to fall asleep next to you and wake up in your arms."

Tucking a strand of hair behind my ear, he smiles. "I had a feeling, and after your surgery, I knew for sure."

"How?"

"That night, you asked me to sleep on the couch—right next to you. You said that's where you wanted me to stay. Every time you've asked me to sleep in your room, you had that same look in your eyes. The desperate need for me to stay."

My voice shakes. "Sometimes I don't understand this. How did it happen so fast? It scares me because what if we're doing everything backward?"

"Then we're doing it backward. But the way I see it, talking before we met was dating. Us spending every night cooking and watching our favorite shows together is building on that. Letting each other see our vulnerable sides is deepening our connection. We've moved fast, but other than restaurant date nights, I don't think we've skipped much. If you want some of those, though,

I'm happy to plan them. In case you haven't figured it out, I'd do just about anything for you."

I laugh a little. "I figured that out when you asked me to marry you the day after we met in person." I run my hands underneath his shirt, reveling in the feeling of his skin against mine. "And I don't need fancy date nights. I just need you. Us." My breath shudders. "This."

He leans in and presses his lips to my neck. "And what does my wife need?"

"To feel you buried inside me."

"Jade," he groans.

"What? I'm getting better at using my words."

"If you talk as dirty to me as your characters do in your books, I'll come without you touching me."

Leaning up, I nip his ear. "Something to try in the future. But for tonight, I need you. I need the physical and emotional all wrapped up together."

His lips land on mine again, and my body goes all tingly and my legs feel like jelly.

Slowly, he breaks our kiss and pulls my shirt over my head before unclasping my bra.

Then he runs his finger down my right arm. "We need to keep this safe." An easy grin appears, and he steps around me. "Finish getting naked while I get the bed ready for you."

A chill rolls through me at his words, but I follow his instructions, dropping my shorts and underwear to the floor.

Carefully, I climb onto the bed, desire pooling inside me. I was thinking his caretaking might ebb now that I'm healing more, but I think it's a part of him. No matter what, he'll take care of me.

My heart beats harder at that.

He's my person.

I'm not sure when it happened, but he became the one I rely on now. More than friendships. More than my dad. More than myself.

I lie down in the center of the bed, and he carefully props my arm up on some pillows, then stands up and strips down.

"I guess this means no rough sex for a bit." He gives me a roguish smile.

"Mm, don't tease me with what I can't have."

He climbs onto the bed with me. "Don't worry, I promise you'll enjoy every second of this."

His thumb rolls over my clit as he pushes two fingers inside me.

"Yes. Justin. Please."

He leans over me, moving his fingers slowly as he kisses my neck.

"Protection."

"I have an IUD. And everything else is good."

"Same. Not the IUD part." We both laugh. He lifts his head, looking into my eyes. "Can I take you bare?"

I bite my lip at the thought. I can't remember the last time I went bare with someone. Maybe my high school boyfriend after I got on birth control.

"God, yes."

He pulls his hand away, and I groan at the lack of contact.

His hot gaze sweeps over me, a troublesome smirk on his lips. "Tell me what you like. What you need."

I nod toward the bedside table. "My clit needs a lot of love. Grab one of my vibrators."

He arches a brow. "*One* of?"

The girlish giggle I let out makes his gaze harden with intensity.

"Open the drawer."

Eyes on me, he pulls it open, and I watch his face as he looks inside.

"Damn, baby. This is quite a collection." He pulls out the biggest one. It's long and slightly cone-shaped with ripples. It's a mix of purple and brown. "What is this?"

I lock eyes with him, completely unashamed. "It's meant to represent the Beast."

He blinks a couple of times. "As in *Beauty and the Beast?*"

"Yep."

"Fuck," he groans. "I can't wait to use this on you. But not tonight." He puts it back and pulls out another. "This one looks like even more fun." He holds up the one that looks sort of like a teardrop and comes to a fine, malleable point that perfectly directs the vibrations. It's one of my favorites and not too bulky for use during sex or with another toy.

He turns it on the lowest setting and gently presses it to my clit.

"Can you get off just like this? Nothing else but these soft vibrations."

"It depends how much you want to tease me. You might need to turn the vibrations up a little."

"Not yet."

He lies down next to me and sucks one of my nipples into his mouth.

The gasp I let out and the way I arch into him makes a rumble of a laugh slip from him.

My nipples are very sensitive and on occasion I've been able to get off on nipple stimulation alone. It's not quite the same level of orgasm, but it still feels incredible. So combining nipple play with the vibrator on my clit...

Moaning, I reach up and tweak the nipple not in his mouth as the vibrator hits the right spot again and again, until—

"Oh," I cry as my orgasm washes over me.

Slowly, Justin pulls the vibrator away and lifts his mouth off me, his face morphing into smug satisfaction.

"Look at how easily you come for me."

He sucks on my neck, then slowly kisses down my chest as my body thrums with desire. Swirling his tongue along the edge of my belly button, he moves lower, kissing across my hips and down to my pelvis. Then he grabs my thighs and lifts them up, sweeping his tongue between my legs and feasting on me.

"Justin…"

"You taste so damn good. I couldn't resist a little snack."

He sucks on my clit one last time, then sits back, roughly fingering me as he strokes his thick cock.

"Please," I whimper.

"Please what, darlin'?"

"I need you inside me before I come again."

He lets out a shuddery breath, then grabs my thighs again. "As you wish, wifey."

CHAPTER TWENTY-FOUR

Justin

JADE'S DRENCHED pussy teases my tip as I line myself up at her entrance.

When she stood in front of me, so vulnerable, asking if this was real, all I wanted was to say the right words to prove to her it is. Now, I need to show her she's mine in every way.

"Once I take this pussy, it belongs to me. No one else will ever touch you again. Understand?"

She stares at me, wide-eyed, then nods fervently.

"Take me. I'm yours. As long as you know it goes both ways. Your cock is now my personal toy. You belong to me."

Those words alone send me flying toward the edge. They're all I've wanted for weeks now. For her to see herself as mine and claim me as hers.

Holding her thighs tightly, I press inside her.

"Fuck... yes," she whines.

"Grab the vibrator and tease your clit. I need to feel you come on my cock this time."

She scrambles for it and turns it on, moaning the second it touches her.

I feel a hint of the vibrations too, and I have to take a second to calm myself down.

Jade wiggles her hips in frustration. "Move."

"One second," I rasp.

After a few deep breaths, I'm back in control and ready to claim what's mine.

I move in and out of her in long, hard strokes. She lets go, giving in to pleasure. I soak in the delicious sounds of her whimpers and moans, but it's the hazy look on her face that has me barreling toward the edge.

"Harder," she breathes.

Hand on the side of her neck and thumb brushing her throat, I drive into her over and over.

"Justin," she whimpers, then she's pulsing around me, and it takes all my effort to hold back my orgasm because I'm not done yet. I still need more. So much more of her.

God, she's stunning like this. Splayed out, beautiful body flushed and trembling from her orgasm, all her soft curves slick with sweat.

She turns the vibrator off and sets it aside, then her eyes lock on mine.

"Flip over."

In my hazy, too-close-to-coming state, her words don't compute. "What?"

"Flip over. I want to ride you."

Oh, fuck.

Rest in peace me. I'm done for.

"Whatever my wife wants."

Though it means I have to pull out of her for a second, which sucks until the cool air hits my wet cock, sending a chill up my spine and making me even harder.

I lie down on my back, and she climbs over the top of me, staring down at me like a predator watching their prey.

She drags her teeth over her bottom lip, and I realize that look is less like a predator and their prey and more like a cat with its toy.

I'll be her toy. I'll be whatever she wants me to be.

"I might need a little help," she whispers, grabbing the headboard with her left hand and lifting her hips. "Since my right hand can't do much."

"Tell me what you need."

"Hold my hips."

I instantly grab them, sinking my fingers into her soft flesh.

"Good boy."

Jesus.

I let out a guttural moan as she slides down my cock.

"Yes, baby. Yes, yes."

She rolls her hips a few times, barely lifting them, then she smiles. A wicked smile as she lifts her hips again and rides me hard.

"Fuck," I cry.

Her moans are long and deep as she fucks me like she owns me.

She does. I'm all hers.

Forever. Or as long as she'll have me.

"Yes, darlin'," I whine. "Yes, yes…"

"Justin," she groans.

Holding her hips tighter, I buck into her, matching her strokes.

She throws her head back, crying out as our bodies slam together.

I'm intoxicated, completely lost in her. I barely notice the tingling in my spine or the way my balls tighten.

"That's it. Come for me. Paint my pussy. Show me I'm yours."

"Fuck." My fingers dig into her hips as I cry out her name, my body going taut as I spill inside her. But then she comes again, and the feel of her squeezing my cock sends me even higher, another orgasm pulsing through me. High-pitched moans are all that come out of me as she rides me until we're both spent.

I hold her trembling body as she climbs off me and settles in next to me, burying her head in my shoulder as she drapes her right arm over me.

"That was incredible. *You* are incredible."

She lifts her head, a sweet yet mischievous smile on her face. "Anything for you, hubby."

That word sets off something inside me. Not heat. Emotion. That's how I want her to see me.

I shift so we're lying face to face, then sweep some hair behind her ear.

"Earlier when you asked if there was something between us, you said our marriage is just legal, but that's not how I feel."

"What do you mean?"

"It might not have happened how a typical marriage does, but I want it to be a marriage. I love living with you, spending time with you, doing all the little domestic things with you, and I love taking care of you. I love being your husband, and that's what I want you to consider me."

My heart is in my hands—actually, it's in *her* hands—as I wait for her answer.

She brings her hand to my cheek, her maple bourbon eyes staring intently into mine.

"You're my husband," she breathes. Then she tosses her leg over mine and snuggles in close again.

I lay flat on my back, pulling her tighter to me and playing with her soft hair.

"And I'm your wife," she whispers, pressing her lips to my neck. "All yours."

With everything inside me, I hope she always will be.

CHAPTER TWENTY-FIVE

Jade

I'M HAPPY.

Like Elizabeth Bennet at the end of *Pride and Prejudice*.

Incandescently happy.

I had my first PT session today, and even though there were some slightly painful moments while testing my range of motion in my fingers, it was so good to be making progress.

My PT told me I can start typing, no more than an hour or two per day to start, but it's something. As much as I wanted to come home and start typing right away, my hand was tired from PT, and overworking it is the last thing I want to do.

But that's okay. Justin and I recorded some more, and I'm settling into it now. I'm getting better at slowing my pace while reading and focusing on my diction—admittedly the most challenging piece for me—while still bringing the emotion. We rerecord stuff a lot, but it's been an incredible learning process that gives me hope for recording the rest of this series.

And it's something I get to do with my husband.

At Justin's request, I'm working harder to stop drawing arbitrary lines and treat him as my husband. Yes, we're still establishing our relationship, but he's made it clear this is where he wants to be, and I'm the one he wants.

I wish I could say those negative thoughts about my weight didn't creep in sometimes. I've been hesitant to post much about us on social media. Until this last week, it felt too much like lying to my readers, but that's not the only reason. I haven't wanted to see the negative comments about someone who looks like Justin being with someone who looks like me.

Plus size men can marry skinny women and it's all good. There are tons of shows with that dynamic out there. But if a plus size woman is with a hot guy or one who is thinner than her, he must be cheating or lying or desperate.

I know that's a reflection of the people making those comments and the society they were raised in, but I was raised in that society too, so those ideals hurt when I have them thrown in my face.

Justin hasn't been shy in posting about us—mostly in his stories. He always tags me, and if there are public comments, I avoid reading them.

And now, I don't want anything to interfere with us building a relationship. I want this to work. I want this to last.

He says it's the last love story I'll ever live, and I've never wanted anything to be more true.

I finish tossing a salad, then grab the magic roasted garlic dressing from the refrigerator. Two heads of roasted garlic? Yes, please.

Justin pulls a tray of wings from the oven, and my mouth waters.

I grab slices of crusty bread, drizzle them with olive oil and add them and some salad to each of our plates.

Justin puts a few wings on each plate, then sets the tray down and kisses me.

"Thanks for making wings."

He kisses me again.

"Thank you for cooking with me," he says.

Another kiss, and this time I wrap my hand around the side of his neck and deepen it until we're standing in the middle of the kitchen, making out, and I'm debating if I want him or food more.

But then his stomach growls and, I swear, mine answers.

We pull apart, laughing, but he gives me another quick peck.

"I fucking love this. This is the life I've wanted for so long. Sharing it with you is more than I dreamed of."

"Keep talking like that and I'll drag you to the bedroom until you scream your husband's name."

That is also very, very good.

It's depressing to admit that before Justin, I'd only ever had transactional sex.

Either a previously agreed upon hookup to get off, or having sex with whomever I was with because I felt like that was what I was supposed to do. Or one of us had the desire, so we did it, even if it was more about sex and less about the connection.

Everything with Justin is about our connection. Whether it's slow and torturous or hard and fast, it's about us, not sex. A couple of nights it's been gentle touching, cuddling, and kissing, and it feels just as good.

I've learned some important lessons—that I knew in theory, but never used in practice—about penetrative sex and orgasms not being the overall goal or destination.

What we have is true intimacy, and I'll never settle for less again.

As we sit down on the couch, and Justin's hand brushes mine, sparks shoot everywhere, and I hope I'll never have to worry about that.

"Would it be okay if we watched the Metros game tonight? I love watching our shows, but the Metros are playing the Revs and that's always an amazing matchup."

"Of course. I love baseball. If you want to watch more games, we absolutely can. I knew you liked the Bandits, and you said you watched games with your dad, but I didn't know you enjoyed baseball too. Let's add that into our rotation. Just another way to get to know you better."

"I don't need to watch every game, but baseball is my favorite sport, so watching more often would be fun."

"Then we will."

He hands me the remote, then picks up his phone and starts typing.

"Are you sure you don't mind?"

"I just told you I enjoy baseball too. I'm looking up the schedule, so I know when the next few games are." He reaches over and squeezes my thigh. "Relax."

"I never want to take more than I give. Or take advantage."

He sets his phone to the side and looks at me.

"This is a partnership. There's no taking advantage. And you give me so much more than you realize." He kisses my cheek. "Now stop overthinking and put on the game."

I lean back against the couch and turn the TV on, quickly finding the game. Justin wraps an arm around my shoulders, and I revel in eating a delicious meal and watching one of my favorite teams with my favorite person.

"THIS APARTMENT IS GORGEOUS." My eyes are wide as I look around Frannie and Mark's spacious top-floor apartment. There's a line of windows along the back wall looking out over the river and filling the space with light.

"Thank you. Mark was beyond frustrated when he found out this space was only used for storage—and used minimally at that. Same with the basement. His finance guy kept saying real estate is a good investment, so he offered to buy the other owner out, and jumped in to renovating the space." She flips a hand through her wavy brown hair. "Well, paying someone to. Now this is ours. There's a gym and laundry area in the basement, and two apartments below us. One that we're hoping to rent out." She looks at Justin playfully. "Since he left us for something better. One of the construction workers rented the other for him and his daughter. Anyway, I'm talking your ear off."

"No, I love hearing about it. This is a beautiful place and such a cute town. Woods Junction is home, but Ida is beautiful."

I look out the opposite window that frames part of the downtown silhouette.

"It is." Frannie's computer, sitting on the coffee table, makes a noise. She sighs. "That'll be Kennedy."

"Why?" Justin asks.

"Because she's miffed that I get to meet Jade first, so she's crashing it. Have a seat."

Justin and I sit down on the couch as Frannie answers the video call.

"Oh my gosh! Finally!"

I laugh as Kennedy's face appears on the computer screen in front of us.

Frannie rolls her eyes. "You couldn't just let me have this, could you? Couldn't let me meet her first."

"Justin has been my best friend for like a billion years now—"

"Ten," Frannie corrects, but Kennedy ignores her.

"It's my right to meet his *wife* first. Plus, I started reading her books first."

I lean over and whisper to Justin. "Is this weird?"

He laughs. "No. This is par for the course with the Baker girls."

I stifle a laugh and look back at the screen.

"Well, I really don't need you to compete over me. Especially about who read my books first. Justin already has the spot of number one superfan, and you'll never replace him."

Kennedy's smile grows. "You're making my little Justin so happy."

"Isn't he like two months older than you?" Frannie asks.

Again, Kennedy ignores her.

"Well, he makes me happy too."

"This is adorable. I need to take a screenshot so I can have a picture of you two together."

"How about I send you pictures?" Justin says.

"As long as they aren't nudes, that's fine by me." A tallish guy with light brown curls sticks his head into the frame. "Hey, Jade. I'm Devon. Nice to meet you."

"You too."

"Oh! I've been meaning to tell you how gorgeous you looked in your wedding dress," Kennedy says.

"She's very excited to meet you," Devon adds.

Justin meets Kennedy's eyes through the screen. "She's happy I'm happy. Just like I'm happy the two of you are happy." He lowers his voice. "And even happier I don't have to hear you banging anymore."

Frannie stifles a laugh.

"I think you mean *singing*," Devon says, mischief dancing in his eyes.

"Yeah. Don't be so dramatic. We were just singing." Kennedy smirks at him.

I laugh at that. "Tough code to crack."

Justin runs his thumb over the back of my neck. "That's what I said. Of course, I also told them how dumb they were for not doing it a lot sooner."

"Hey, we can't all move as fast as the Millenium Falcon," Devon says.

I laugh at that. "Are you a *Star Wars* nerd too?"

Devon's gaze flits to Justin. "Not like he is, but I like to use words he understands."

When I glance at Justin, he's staring back at Devon, having some sort of silent conversation with him.

Then he jumps back in. "Okay, this has been fun, but we're going to grab coffee with Frannie, so…"

"Fine," Kennedy says. "But you better come out and visit soon."

Justin glances at me. "We have a reader event in Seattle in September. Maybe we could pop down after?"

I smile at them through the screen. "I would love to."

"Perfect. Oh, and if you're interested, I run a book club out here and I'd love to introduce them to your books."

"That would be amazing. Thank you."

"Of course! I'll text you with more details."

"Sounds good. Take care. It was good to meet you both."

"You too. Bye."

The call disconnects, and Frannie lets out a sigh. "Now that we're done with those shenanigans, it's time for coffee. And maybe some alcohol. Midday drinking is a thing, right?"

I stare hard at her for a minute. "I'm not giving you any spoilers."

"Gah! You're mean. This friendship is already going downhill."

Frannie's gaze turns to Justin, who wraps his arm tightly around my waist. "Sorry. I'm firmly on my wife's team."

And damn if that doesn't make me all melty for him.

A genuine smile grows on Frannie's face. "I guess I can forgive the lack of spoilers if you keep making him smile like that."

"Frannie…" Justin complains.

"Nope. It's my job as your sister-like-person to annoy you and tease you and be absolutely thrilled when you find love. Don't pretend you weren't happy for me."

"Still am."

"Love's really working its way through the friend group," Frannie says.

My eyes widen a little, but Justin wraps his other arm around me too, squeezing me from behind.

Frannie's making her way across the room toward the entryway and doesn't realize what she said, but I heard it.

Justin didn't deny it.

But at this point, I'm not sure I could either.

I think I'm falling in love with my husband.

THIS IS IT.

After three long weeks of pain, frustration, and poor left-handed typing, my laptop is on my lap, raised up by a thick pillow so my hands are perfectly aligned with the keys.

Justin sets a glass of iced tea on the table in front of me, then sits down, leaving a little space between us so I have room to move.

"Need anything else?"

I shake my head, then take a deep breath and open the document for book nine.

I'm so ready to get this story out of my head.

With a deep breath, I reach out with my right hand and start typing.

It's a little strange. My fingers are shaky, and I can't type as fast as I could before, but I'm typing. No pain. No aches. No tightness. No tingling.

The first chapter pours out of me, and though my hand is tired and shaky by the time I'm finished, I fucking did it. I've got my world back.

Tears fill my eyes as I set my laptop aside and massage my palm like the PT and my doctor recommended.

Justin scooches closer, swiping his thumb over my cheek and wiping away a tear.

"What's wrong? Are you in pain?"

"No. No pain. None at all. I wrote a whole chapter."

He lets out a relieved laugh. "That's great."

I turn to him, overwhelmed with gratitude and happiness.

"You don't understand. A little over a month ago, I left the doctor's office in tears, and I couldn't conceive of this moment. I was terrified I'd lose my ability to do this—or at the very least, lose some of my momentum. Then I found out my insurance company wouldn't cover it, and it was a gut punch to have to push off doing audio for this series—these books I really believe in. Then you showed up. Not only did you do something completely crazy to make sure I wouldn't have to put one of my dreams on hold, you stepped in. You took care of me. I'm so grateful for this moment, but I'm even more grateful that you are by my side while I experience it."

"Jade." His voice is thick with emotion. He shakes his head, then takes my face in his hands and kisses me soft and slow. When he pulls away, he brushes his nose against mine. "It's an honor to be the one at your side."

He wraps me in a hug, and I hold him tightly, needing him to know how much he means to me.

Love is born in seconds, but grows over a lifetime.

Now I know, without a doubt, it grows between us a little more each day.

CHAPTER TWENTY-SIX

Justin

"THIS IS AMAZING!" Jade's smile could light up the entire stadium as she looks around the home of the New York Metros.

When she told me how much she loved them, I texted the football guys to see if one of them could swing tickets for us. I figured we had a better chance of getting good seats if I asked them. They may be different sports, but they're still New York sports. Plus, it turns out Mark actually knows the Metros newest pitcher, Jamie Henderson. I guess his cousin is one of his friends.

"Thank you for doing this." Jade leans in and kisses my cheek.

"Of course."

"What are we? Chopped liver?" Mark asks.

The guys are all on their off day from training camp and, along with Frannie and Hallie, met up with us for the game.

"I appreciate you getting the tickets for us. But... he knew I wanted them."

Mark shakes his head and sighs. "Fair. I get it. That's what good partners do."

"Magically know what their girls need?" A voice comes from behind us.

Mark stands up, smiling. "Hey, Mands."

Jade and I turn in our seats and see a curvy girl with long strawberry blonde hair.

"Wait, Amanda?" Jade asks.

She turns to Jade, eyes wide. "Jade?"

Mark and I share a bewildered look as Jade stands up and they share a quick hug.

"I didn't even think about you being here," Jade says, glancing over at the field.

Mark waves a hand. "How do you two know each other?"

"Amanda is also from Woods Junction. We met for the first time years ago when she came to one of my signings. She's come to almost every local one since then, even after getting all her books signed."

Amanda shrugs. "I like to support other badass women."

Jade smiles brightly at her. "Last year, she was wearing a jersey for the Metros triple A team, and since my dad and I used to have season tickets there when I was a teen, I asked her about it and found out her boyfriend was their pitcher. He's on the Metros now."

"Jamie Henderson," I say, putting all the pieces together.

Mark holds up a hand. "Wait a sec. That means you've totally met my cousins too." He looks at Amanda. "I know you've all gone to signings together."

Jade's eyes get even wider as Amanda nods.

"Yep. Rae, Sarah, and Dani."

Jade slowly shakes her head. "It's a small world."

"That's the shit I love about small towns," I say.

Amanda smiles at me. "Yeah, me too."

"Are you sitting with us?" Mark asks.

"Did you think I'd get you tickets and not hang out? I might need you to move so I can sit next to my author bestie and get spoilers from her." Amanda winks at Jade and Jade laughs.

I wrap my arm around the back of her chair, happiness growing inside me.

Maybe it's nothing. A totally stupid idea. But before I ever contacted her or knew she existed, we had this connection to each other. The romance nerd in me wants to get swept up in that and believe we're here because we're destined to be.

All this time, fate was weaving the threads of our lives together, so one way or another, we'd find each other.

This woman was meant to be mine, and there's no doubt in my mind she's the one for me.

I LOOK AROUND MCGILLS TAVERN. The same bar I went to with my friends for years. The same bar we sat at a little over a month ago when Jade and I had first started texting.

So much has changed in such a short time, but I wouldn't change a second of it.

Mark and Frannie went back to their apartment after the game so they could have some time together, and after Jade traded numbers with Amanda, they promised to meet up when Amanda is back home next.

Home.

I went to the DMV a few days ago and got my New York license. Well, I renewed it. Technically, I had one from when I lived there years ago, even though I rarely drove. It has Jade's address on it. *My* address.

I haven't told Jade yet, partly because I want to surprise her, but also because I can tell a part of her is still scared to admit how real this is. Not because she doesn't want it but because she's afraid of getting hurt.

Which I understand. I didn't make my intentions clear enough at the beginning because I didn't want to scare her. Now, I'm doing everything I can to help her see she's all I want. I can tell she wants to ask why, but I don't even want to dignify that potential question with a response.

Those are her insecurities talking, and I refuse to let them get in the way.

She's beautiful, brilliant, witty, playful, and the worlds she can create in her mind and the stories she can tell astound me. I'm the luckiest man alive that she wants me too.

And I just want to love her. It's as simple as that.

As simple as love.

That word has been popping up both internally and externally a lot lately.

We're headed there, no doubt. I've never been as twisted up in someone as I am in her. She doesn't seem to see the way she supports me, cares for me, and brings me joy. Maybe because it's often in the softest, simplest ways, but she does it all and more.

"Love is not coming for me," Hallie says firmly.

Still my little anti-love girl.

"Baby girl, I don't think you get to choose that," Hardy says.

"He's right," Brian says, voice soft, almost haunted.

Hardy looks at him tenderly, and I elbow Jade.

She squeezes my thigh, though we try not to openly stare at them.

"You will find it when the time is right. When the person is right," Hardy says to him.

Brian smiles, but it's almost... bitter. Which is strange for him. He's usually the gentlest, kindest person in the room.

He grabs his drink and downs it, and everything else disappears. The smile he gives Hardy is genuine. "Yeah. You're right. And I don't need to mope, so let's go grab another drink."

Hallie lets them out of the booth, but as she's sitting back down, her eyes go to the door, and she watches as a tall guy with dark hair and a scruffy jaw, dressed in suit pants and a dress shirt —and looking like he'd like to rip them off—walks in.

Hallie sits down, a troublesome smile on her face. "Now *that* is what I want to fall into."

I nod toward the bar. "Go make your move."

She arches a brow. "Please. Have you forgotten how this works? I have to let him see me as I walk by first, then I'll go get a drink, brush his arm..."

Jade laughs. "You have a system."

"Yep."

I glance over at Hardy and Brian at the bar.

"Random question—"

"I don't know what's going on, but yes, I think there's something," Hallie says. "The way Brian talks sometimes... I think he has feelings for Hardy."

"But Hardy is oblivious," Jade says.

"Well, maybe it leads to a bi-awakening situation," I say.

Hallie's brow furrows. "Not everyone is a living romance trope."

Jade laughs and shakes her head as I set my gaze on Hallie.

"People are living, breathing tropes, and romance is just a piece of that. Frannie and Mark are instant connection. Devon and Kennedy, the classic best friends to lovers—"

"One of my favorites," Jade says. Then she gestures between the two of us. "Marriage of convenience."

Hallie crosses her arms over her chest, looking smug. "What's mine then?"

Jade and I look at each other, and I gesture for her to say it.

"Afraid to love."

Hallie squints at her, then downs the rest of her beer and climbs out of the booth, shaking her head. "Romance people," she mutters as she walks away.

Jade and I clink our glasses together and laugh.

WE WAVE goodbye to Hardy and Brian as they leave.

As much as they would've loved to hang out all night, they have to get their asses kicked for the last few days of training camp and need some rest.

I could use some rest too.

Alone in the hotel room with Jade.

I glance over at the bar, where Hallie is being touchy and flirty. She's in the final stage of her plan, and if it works, Jade and I can go soon.

We have a strict rule that we don't leave without having a quick meeting with any potential hookup, so we know whoever it is will be safe.

As Hallie leans away from the bar, the guy slides off his stool.

"Oh, incoming," Jade says.

I take a sip of my drink, pretending not to watch them as they walk over to us, hand in hand and laughing.

Time for me to play my part. Standing up, I slip into my older brother role, which is always convincing since we both have a similar shade of blond hair, and I can pull off menacing.

"This is who I have to get approval from?" he asks.

"I'm Justin, the older brother. The guys who just left are the two professional football players that'll help me hide your body if you hurt her." I look at Hallie. "Location on?"

"Yep. Shared with you."

"Good. Now, for posterity…" I pull out my phone and snap a picture of him. "Turn to the side." He stares at me for a moment, then the ghost of a smile crosses his face and he does it. I snap another photo. "Thank you…"

"Deck," he says.

I almost snort at that, then give him one more menacing look. He holds up his hands. "We're not doing full names, but I don't have a secret identity, I promise. With my picture, you can find me. I won't hurt her."

There's something surprisingly earnest in his voice. Maybe he has a younger sister too, so he gets it.

Then he looks back at Hallie. "Ready to go, Hells Bells?"

I glance at Jade. *Hells Bells?* she mouths.

Hallie just puts a finger to her lips.

"I'll text you that I'm alive later."

"You better," I say, keeping my voice extra low and growly as a reminder to *Deck* that I'm not fucking around.

"Let's go," she whispers, leaning in close to him.

He wraps his hand tightly around hers, and with a wave, they leave the bar.

I turn back to Jade, who smiles up at me. "Does that mean we can go now too?"

Offering my hand, I help her out of the booth, then squeeze her ass. "It's about damn time."

"YES," Jade whines as I stroke her clit and finger her pussy.

She's doing her nightly hand strengthening exercises. Stroking my cock.

She sucks on my neck, and my breath shudders.

"I'm close," I groan.

"Move your fingers faster."

I do as she asks, and a moment later, she's pulsing around my fingers and crying out.

Shifting, I climb on top of her. This is my favorite way to finish lately.

She strokes me faster, then with her left hand, she gives my balls a little squeeze.

"Fuck," I groan, my abs tightening.

"Come on, baby. Come all over me. Mark me. Show me who I belong to."

"Jade... fuck..." I force my eyes open long enough to watch my cum paint her perfect tits.

She laughs as she releases me, licking the bit of my cum off her fingers.

Lying down next to her, I kiss her deeply, tasting myself on her tongue. A thrill goes through me at that. The evidence that I've claimed her. She's my girl.

We break our kiss when she yawns, and with a firm slap to her ass, I send her to get cleaned up.

Quickly checking my phone, I find a text from Hallie that she's safely back at her apartment and will message me in the morning. I have a feeling she's not alone, but there's security in the building there twenty-four-seven, so I'm not too worried.

Jade switches off the lamp as she climbs back into bed naked and curls her body around mine, every perfect curve molding to my hard body.

"Today was amazing. Thank you," she murmurs, guiding me to her lips.

It would be so easy to deepen our kiss and go for round two, but she still needs to rest and heal.

"You don't need to thank me. Seeing you happy is all I need."

She's quiet for a long moment as I stroke my fingers through her hair.

"Back at you," she whispers, popping a kiss on my cheek. "Goodnight."

"I... uh, goodnight."

I hold her tighter, my heart slamming into my ribs. Because I almost... I wanted to say...

I love you.

The words fill my heart.

I'm not sure if I'm ready to say them yet, but I know with certainty, they're the truth.

CHAPTER TWENTY-SEVEN

Jade

I'VE GOT my groove back.

It's been a month and a half since my surgery, and things are going well.

My mobility and range of motion has increased in my fingers. Still no pain at all. And I can make a fist again. I still can't do anything that requires me to be weight bearing with my hand, and I've gotten good at opening jars and bottles with my left hand, but otherwise, I'm getting back to normal.

Most importantly, I'm typing several hours a day again, and book nine is flying out of me.

So much so that I'm letting the itch to work on my secret project take over. For years, it's been my catharsis. Something just for me. My safe place, and the project that speaks to my soul—the girl who grew up loving Disney Princesses and fairytales. It's been a few years, and every so often I consider querying them, but I always second-guess myself.

They're special to me. And having them stomped on scares me. But if I ever want to share them with the world, I'll have to get over that because whether I try for the traditional route or self-publish, criticism will come my way. I'm getting closer, though.

When I was at my most bored, I went back and read the first two books and was pleasantly surprised they weren't nearly as bad as I'd convinced myself they were. I'm planning to spend some time next week editing them, but I would be comfortable letting some trusted sources beta read them.

Today though, I'm working on book five. A twist on *Snow White and the Huntsman*. Only there are three huntsmen and no dwarves. One of the huntsmen is looking for her. She ends up shacking up with all three of them, and the one who is supposed to turn her in is fighting all his instincts. I'm at the climactic part now where he finally reveals who he is, and she tries to run, but they keep her there, promising fealty to her, then tying her to the bed and worshipping her. There might be some sword crossing action too.

But for this bit particularly, they'll all be focused on her.

And she's going to be filled up.

I wiggle in my spot at the corner of the couch and instantly feel Justin's gaze on me.

"Okay over there, wifey?"

I clear my throat. Am I going to tell him what I'm thinking? Or even about the project?

I think I want to. At least the project. Maybe the other stuff.

"Uh... just working on something a little different, and thinking about it."

He slides closer. "Different how?"

"It's male-male-male-female."

His eyes widen. "Oh, really? Not part of the Marianos, then?"

I slowly shake my head. "This is my secret project. Like super secret. No one else knows about it."

"Will you tell me?" His words are gentle and encouraging.

"Okay, so you know my lore is fairytales and Disney Princesses. This is a series of retellings."

"How many books?"

"I'm on the fifth, and I have plans for the sixth."

His eyes light up. "What are they? I need to know more. Also, can I read them?"

I laugh at that. "I think I might be ready to let someone read the first two."

"I volunteer as tribute."

"I thought you might. Anyway, the first is *Beauty and the Beast*. Second is a sapphic version of *Sleeping Beauty*. Third is *Cinderella*. Fourth is a male-male *Little Mermaid*. The sixth one will be *Peter Pan*. And the one I'm working on right now is a polyamorous *Snow White and the Hunts*men. Three men and Snow White." I swallow hard.

He quirks a brow, heat settling in his gaze. "And what about that has my sweet little romance author squirming?"

I sink my teeth into my bottom lip. "I'm writing a scene where they all take her. And I want to know... what it would be like. Not being with multiple people. But..." I scrub my hands over my face as my cheeks burn, but Justin reaches over and pulls my hands away.

"Tell me."

"When I've written male-male stuff, I don't have a frame of reference for what anal would feel like for a man any more than what coming feels like for a man, so I read other books and had queer male beta readers. I know I don't have to know what it's like to write it. I can research and talk to women who have experienced it, but—"

"You want to know. It's okay to want to explore that."

"I more than want to. I'm *desperate*."

"Turn that off," Justin growls, gesturing to my laptop.

I scramble to do it. Then he's yanking me off the couch and leading me to the bathroom.

"Since you've never done this before, I'll help you prep. I

don't have a ton of experience, but I've done it a few times and know what needs to be done."

I suck in a shaky breath.

"It's okay if you're nervous. And if you want to stop at any point, say the word and we will."

I nod, body trembling with both anticipation and nerves.

Standing in the middle of the bathroom, Justin strips me down, and when he gets to my underwear, he groans. "Christ, darlin'. These are soaked."

"I told you," I moan as he kisses my neck.

Then his hand comes down on my ass in a crisp smack. I whine in response.

"I can't wait to take this perfect ass. But first, let's get you prepped."

Justin takes me through an entire routine, starting in the shower, then moving to the bedroom, where he uses the anal vibrator I bought but never used to help get me ready. It's unsettling at first, but as I relax, it feels amazing, and I'm craving more. I need him.

I'm lying on my side on the bed, my right hand resting on a pillow, with Justin behind me.

"Tell me exactly what you want," he rumbles.

"I want the super thin clit stimulator. I can hold that with my left hand. Then I want a toy for my pussy... and you for—"

He sinks his mouth over mine in a rough kiss.

"What toy do you want?"

I lock eyes with him, and he instantly knows.

The Beast.

He pulls it from the drawer and squirts some lube on it, then hands me the clit stimulator.

"I'm going to start slow," he rasps.

Since this one is tapered, it gives a little more control over how much I take.

"Wait. I want you inside me first. I care more about that than the toy."

He lets out a shuddery breath. "As you wish, darlin'."

Turning my head, I watch as he squirts some lube onto his cock and strokes himself.

I've never been more turned on in my life. I'm nervous, but I want to know what it feels like.

"I'm going to take this very slow."

He squirts more lube into his hand, then carefully pulls the vibrator out. The sudden emptiness has me wiggling my ass toward Justin.

"Patience."

The cool lube is a jolt to my senses, but when he presses his finger against my hole, I relax again.

A moment later, the head of his cock is there, and I have to turn the clit stimulator off because I'm too close to coming. I want the whole experience.

"Do it," I plead.

And slowly—torturously fucking slowly—he presses his tip inside. I bear down and breathe, taking him deeper.

"Just like that, baby," he groans.

"Ah, fuck. Holy... shit."

"Is that good or bad?"

"Good. I need more."

Grabbing my hip, he holds me steady as he works his way in.

"Yes," I cry.

The deeper he gets, the less my brain works, and it's all nonsense and noises.

"How do you feel?" he asks once he's fully seated inside me.

"So good. I want more. Use the toy."

He lets out a restrained groan, then nips at my shoulder.

"This might kill me."

He swirls the tip of the toy around my entrance, slowly pushing it in. My vision goes blurry. No wonder the women in those books are so damn happy to take all the dicks. I couldn't imagine doing this every day, but sometimes... *fuck*. It's incredible. Overwhelming. It's hard to breathe, but I need more.

"Look at how much you can take." Justin's groan is sinful as he pulls the toy out a little, then pushes it back in farther.

"Yes. Just like that. I—I need you to move. Please."

He gets the toy a little farther in, then takes a big breath and slips part way out before pushing back in.

I clench the sheets and turn the vibrator on, shakily moving it between my legs.

Justin wraps one leg around mine and kisses my back as he moves in and out, then he moves the toy in sync with the motion of his hips.

"Oh my god. Fuck. Yes. Faster. Please."

He picks up his pace, and I scream with pleasure, completely overcome.

My clit tingles and my stomach warms, but the feeling of pleasure is different. Bigger than an orgasm.

"Oh my—yes—I—I..." I cry out, as a different kind of pleasure ripples through me and I feel like I'm going to pee, and then... oh. Shit. I'm squirting everywhere.

"Oh, yes," Justin groans, holding me tighter.

"Fuck," I whine. Still so overwhelmed in the best way.

I've played with plenty of toys, but I've never squirted before, and now... now...

"I'm going to..."

Justin lifts his head and watches me squirt this time, barely suppressing a groan.

"Faster."

"I'm barely holding on, baby," he rasps. "Your ass keeps squeezing the life out of my cock. I'm too close to coming."

"So am I. Don't hold back. Please. I need to feel this. I'm so full. So perfectly full. Now I need a little more."

Holding me tighter, he moves faster, and for a second, I swear I go blind. I bury my face in the blankets, moaning into them as I'm double fucked.

"Yes, yes..." Haze filters over me and warmth blooms in my stomach. "Justin," I cry out loudly as I come.

"Fuck." Justin buries his head in my neck. "Jade..."

He moans loudly in my ear as his warmth fills me. I'm coming all over again, my abs so tight I can barely breathe.

"Holy fuck," I pant, tossing the vibrator to the side. I've never felt more empowered or confident. And that was a whole new realm of what sex and intimacy can be.

Justin kisses across my shoulder. "That was..." He trails off, at a loss for words.

"Mhm," I agree.

I tilt my head so I can kiss him, and his hot mouth on mine while he's still buried deep inside me has me ready to go again.

Or maybe not. I'm not sure I can move.

Slowly, Justin slips out of me, then removes the toy, and the feeling of fullness fades. It's not that I want it back right now, but I also feel empty without it.

My breath shakes, and it takes a few minutes for me to get a good, deep breath in.

"We should clean up," Justin whispers.

I nod, but it takes us a few minutes to get off the bed.

Eventually, we end up back in the shower. Though it only takes Justin a few minutes to clean off, I take longer, making sure I feel okay everywhere and I'm fully cleaned off.

When I get back to the bedroom, I find Justin has cleaned up the blankets he put down as a barrier and changed the sheets. Even though it's only the middle of the afternoon, he's under the covers waiting for me.

I join him and our naked bodies instantly collide as we kiss.

I've never come so hard in my life, and I should be fully sated, but the new experience has left me keyed up, ready for more.

Justin gently bites my lip as he pulls away. "Did you enjoy that?"

With a laugh, I nod. "Definitely. Did you? Because I really want to do that again."

"Thank fuck. It was so hot. "

He kisses me hard.

"Thank you," I murmur against his lips. "For making me feel safe enough to try that."

"Thank you for letting me be your safe place."

We stare at each other for a moment, the words neither of us has said, dancing through the air.

"I..." But the words don't come out, so I dive forward and kiss him again, showing him the words I can't say, how much I care for him, and how grateful I am for him.

How much I love him.

"You're mine, darlin'. Mine."

Then he's buried deep inside me, my pussy swelling around his cock as we give in to the depth of emotions overtaking us.

My fragile, romantic heart beats steadily with the words I can't stop thinking.

I hope this lasts forever.

CHAPTER TWENTY-EIGHT

Jade

LAZY SATURDAY MORNINGS are my favorite thing.

We get up late and have bagels and coffee in bed while we get work done.

I'm almost finished with book nine. This is the fastest I've written a book in years, but it helps that I had the entire thing plotted in my head and extensive voice notes to help me remember exactly what I wanted to say in some climactic moments.

It's crazy that it's been two months since Justin and I met in person and my entire life changed, but I'm happier now than I knew I could be.

Mostly. We're still dancing around the *L-word*, but I need to just woman up and say it. I don't know if I'm afraid to break our bubble or if I'm that desperate to hear him say it first, but not communicating never got anyone anywhere.

Does that magically make me good at it? Nope.

Both our phones go off a couple of times, and I glance over at mine, not wanting to answer and interrupt my flow, but it's been driving me nuts all morning. They've been going off here and there. It's probably the group chat since no one has called, but I'll get sucked into a conversation if I answer that.

Justin sighs and closes his laptop, then leans over to kiss me.

"I'm going to take a shower. Consider this your twenty-minute warning, because I'm taking you out for brunch when I'm done."

I smile at him. "Okay, hubby."

He makes a whiny noise and kisses my neck.

"Don't do that."

I can't help but laugh. "Sorry. I forgot how much you like it when I call you that."

"Mhm. Somehow, I doubt that."

He climbs off the bed and grabs his phone, mumbling something to himself about seeing what all the hubbub is.

He makes some kind of strangled noise, and I look up, brow furrowing. He's standing by the bed, staring at his phone, reading rapidly.

"What the fuck?" he mutters.

"What is it?"

His gaze snaps to me, and he sits back down.

"This fucking guy..."

I shut my laptop and set it aside. "What? What is it?"

"Darren Corval."

"The skeevy influencer guy?"

"Yeah. You know he got banned from a couple more reader events?"

I nod. Stories about him have been making their way around author circles, and a couple of events dropped him from the allegations about them. Some are much worse than what he did to me.

Justin huffs out a sigh. "Well, he's trying to take the heat off himself."

"What do you mean?"

Reluctantly, he hands me his phone.

"He's tried to say some things about me in some author circles, but I wasn't worried about it. No one was buying it anyway. Apparently, he needed to kick things up a notch."

My mouth drops as I read what the creep posted social media this morning.

Social media can be disgusting. These last few weeks have been nothing but a witch hunt, and I'm tired. Tired of being quiet, and especially not naming names about who started all of this. But it's time for me to protect myself and expose the lying frauds who began this disinformation campaign against me.

Justin Ayers and Jade Jackson.

Justin is far from the golden boy everyone knows him as, and Jade is a money-hungry famewhore.

It shouldn't be a surprise to anyone to learn that their marriage is a sham. All done for publicity to increase Jade's book sales and Justin's exposure. They've taken advantage of their fans and new readers alike for their own gains.

I met up with Jade two nights before their supposed marriage, and if she was so in love with Justin, why did she have her hands all over me? When Justin saw, he threatened me, then they made up a story to cover their own asses. Their scam of a marriage is so pathetically see through, I'm shocked no one else has poked holes in it yet.

It's ridiculous they even tried to fool anyone. All it takes is one look to see they clearly don't fit together. Someone like her ending up with someone who looks like him? Please.

It's unfortunate that they've tried to play games with their readers. In the end, who they really are will come to light, but I couldn't stay quiet any longer.

The truth will prevail.

-D

I'm going to throw up.

I'm shaking with fury and absolute dread.

He's accusing us? And there are so many likes on his post. So many people stepping up to defend him, who, in their comments say, they've never even heard of us.

Fuck him.

But also... what do we do? The urge to check all my sales dashboards is strong.

How will this affect my life? My livelihood? Justin's?

I turn to him, mouth agape.

"Breathe," he says gently. "It'll be okay."

"How? The things he said—"

"Are lies."

"And no one has ever believed a lie before. What's that saying? Lies travel around the world before the truth can get its shoes on?"

"Yeah. And eventually that lie ends up tired and worn through. The truth is still strong and steady. We did nothing wrong, and we have plenty of people who can back us up on that. I'll go back to that hotel bar and find that bartender. He saw even more than I did."

I shake my head. "This could destroy our careers."

"I really don't believe it will at all. The people who are going to buy his shit weren't people who were ever going to support us anyway. He's angry, and he's lashing out. That's what people do when they're cornered. The truth is coming for him. I know female authors and influencers who have had issues with him. All it takes is the trickle of information to start and people will come forward."

His words don't settle me at all.

"What do we do now?"

"We get ready and go to brunch. Later, we can make a joint post, not combating his lies, but clarifying our relationship. Then, as he said, we let the truth prevail. Because it will."

I gape at him. "You're serious? You want me to go to brunch right now?"

He nods vigorously. "Yes. Because he wins if his words hold you back. He wins if his words sideline us. We're going to keep living and being us. We have nothing to prove."

But we do, don't we? I mean, our careers are on the line. At least to some degree. The urge to stand up and scream out a defense is driving me right now.

"Trust me," he whispers. "I'm going to shower. Want to join me? I'll distract you."

He gives me a sweet little smirk, but that's all way too much right now. My mind is still reeling.

"Uh... I'm just... going to get ready. I'll get ready."

He leans in and kisses my cheek. "It's going to be okay."

Then he's up and across the room.

The second the bathroom door is closed, I lunge for my phone, then go back and read his post again. But I don't stop there. I do the truly stupid thing and open the comments. I read a few on Justin's phone, but this is... a hellscape. Sure, there are a few people defending us, but there are loads more who have decided I'm now an author they'll never read, and so many people are saying they'll never listen to another book Justin narrates and it's time to burn the books where he's on the cover.

It's horrifying.

I check my sales dashboard and it's a typical day, but these things can change quickly.

I'm sick to my stomach.

What the fuck do we do?

I manage to get off the bed, but rather than go to the closet, I pace. And read more comments.

If they're not married, she's destroying his life. She has less to lose. No one even knows who she is. If they are married, he's cheating. Who'd want to be stuck with her?

It's those words that stick with me as I look at the bathroom door.

He did so much for me, and all I'm doing for him is ruining his career. One he built for a decade before he met me.

My phone vibrates in my hand, and I almost throw it across the room. But then I see it's my group text with Zoey and Trish.

ZOEY

Are you okay?

TRISH

If you need to come over and vent, we're at Zo's.

I glance back at the bathroom door. Justin said it's going to be fine, but I'm not so sure about that. I need to figure out what I'm thinking and how I want to handle it all.

On my way.

CHAPTER TWENTY-NINE

Justin

DARREN CORVAL CAN EAT shit and die.

I practically scrubbed my skin raw in the shower with how angry I am. Not because he said shit about me. What the fuck ever. I lived through the New York modeling scene. If I couldn't handle guys like him, I never would've survived. But he said shit about Jade, and that makes the psychotic, *I-want-to-put-him-in-a-shallow-grave* side of me come out.

Don't go after my wife.

I've already been in contact with my cousin Stacy about what we need for a defamation lawsuit, just in case.

We aren't there yet, and I doubt anything will come of this before it goes softly into the night. It's such a load of trash and the people who feed off that are trolls.

I meant what I said to Jade. It'll blow over and be okay. I'm determined to distract her as much as possible until she's a little calmer, and then we can figure out what we want to post.

I run my hand through my wet hair, spiking it up a little, then open the door to the bedroom.

"Baby, I hope you're wearing a short little dress, because—"

I cut off when I find the room empty.

"Jade?"

I wander out to the living room and kitchen, but she isn't there, either.

What the hell?

Spinning on my heel, I run down to the office, my heart ticking up when she's not there. As I turn to leave the room, my eye catches the window and her car isn't in the driveway.

Pulling my phone from my pocket, I run out to the living room and call her.

Voicemail.

My stomach burns.

Where would she be? Why did she leave?

Breathe.

When my phone rings, I almost drop it, but I right myself, only to see it's not her calling, but her dad.

"Hello?"

"Hey, Justin. I saw that post on social media this morning. How are you? How's Jade? She wasn't answering her phone when I called."

Sighing, I drop onto the couch. "She's not answering for me either. I showed her the post this morning, and we talked. I went to take a shower—now she's gone. I don't know where she is. I'm guessing not with you."

He hums. "No. She's not. If I had to guess, she's panicking. Losing what she's worked so hard for is her greatest fear. And when she feels like she's in trouble, she wants to fight back, prove herself. If I had to guess where she went, I'd say Trish's or Zoey's."

"Probably Zoey's," I grit out.

But why? Why did she leave me? We're supposed to be a team. Figure it out together.

"She's still getting used to having you to rely on, son. Don't stress too much. Find her and talk to her."

"Papa Jackson, can you read minds?"

He laughs. "No. But I know my daughter. And I know the way you care for her—and it's been obvious from day one that you've wanted to make this last. Which is how I know you will."

I let out a weak laugh and run my hand over my face. "Thanks."

"No problem. Call if you need anything."

"I will. Bye."

He hangs up, and I lean back against the couch.

I hate that she ran from me, but it's only been two months. There's still a lot to learn about each other. There's still trust to build. That's okay.

I stare down at my phone, then unlock the screen and open my notes app, so I can type out a post. I need to do this before I go find my wife.

It takes me a half hour and lots of backspacing before I have something I'm happy with. I open one of my social media apps and the first thing I do is upload photos. A whole slideshow of them. All sweet little moments of Jade and me. A selfie from after her surgery, then a bunch of selfies of us from the last few weeks, then a photo Hallie sent me of Jade and I kissing at the Metros game, and for the last picture I put the kiss from our wedding. A moment so raw and real it's impossible to deny our love.

Then I add the text.

I usually don't comment on hearsay and gossip, but this morning my wife was ruthlessly attacked, and I won't sit by and allow it.

A predatory man was behind those words. And I say predatory because despite his delusional claims that my wife was all over him, their only point of contact was when he sexually assaulted her by grabbing her ass. I witnessed her horror at being touched without consent, but I wasn't the only one. Several patrons in the bar and the bartender witnessed this. The bartender saw even more than I did. There is a reason that person has been removed from events and it wasn't a smear campaign.

Talking about him is the last thing I want to do on this or any day.

I'd much rather tell you about my wife. And yes, I know I call her "my wife" too much. She rolls her eyes about it. But I'm not going to stop because I'm acutely aware of how lucky I am.

Our story has been a whirlwind. I slipped into her DMs to gush about one of her books, only to fall head over heels for her during our daily conversations. Our all day conversations. Getting married in Las Vegas was fast, but it was not done on a whim. Her father wouldn't have been there if that was the case. The truth is, I've known in my soul from the moment we started speaking that Jade Jackson and her beautiful heart were meant to be mine. I'm honored to be the one to protect her and her heart, though I wish I didn't have to. She is kind, talented, brilliant, and funny. She's a bright light, and I'm damn lucky that she saw even a shred of those things in me. With her, I'm finally home.

Jade never posted about us because she didn't want to draw too much attention. She didn't want to feel she was using me. But I can't and won't stop shouting about how much I adore my wife, and how lucky I am that we found each other.

The pictures I've posted speak for themselves. She can write a love story. I can narrate one. But we can't fake love, and we'd never want to.

I read it over one last time, then post it.
Now it's time to go find my wife.

PAPA JACKSON GAVE me Zoey's address, and I'm unsurprised when I pull in the driveway and find Jade's car here. Since Zoey is single and Trish lives with her very overprotective fiancé, who is also Zoey's friend, I assumed that wasn't where she'd end up.

Zoey's house is a beautiful log-cabin home. It's something I might've imagined for myself one day, but now home is that upstairs apartment and the back porch that looks out on the park. I'd love to turn it back into a single-family one day if we ever have kids, but right now, it's all we need.

It's home.

It's where Jade should be.

I knock loudly on Zoey's door, and when it swings open, she and Trish are standing in front of me.

"Where is my wife?"

Zoey looks at Trish. "Why does this keep happening to me? Different house, but same thing. Growly guy storming my front door looking for his girl."

Trish stifles a laugh.

I don't know what the fuck they're talking about, and I really don't care.

"Jade?"

Zoey swings the door all the way open, and I walk in, finding Jade standing in the kitchen.

"Hi."

"We need to talk."

"There's a nice back deck," Trish says.

Jade sighs and nods, leading me out the back door and across the expansive deck. There's a wide staircase, and she sits down on the top stair, looking dejected.

I take a spot a few feet from her and look over at her.

"Why did you leave?"

Her eyes find mine. "I panicked. I read what he said again and started reading through the comments. All the awful things people said. How they would never support you again. I don't want your career to be ruined because you're stuck with me."

I move closer and grab her arm. "Why would you ever think I'm stuck with you? Do you not understand how much you've given me?"

She sniffs and shakes her head, looking down. "I know you wanted a home. You wanted someone to love. But did you actually want *me*?"

Holy fuck. It did not for one goddamn second occur to me that she'd think that.

I rest my palm on her cheek and turn her so she's facing me again. "*You* are the person I love. *You* are my home. Not an apartment or a town. You. Always you. Only you. My home is where your heart is."

She sniffs again, tears trickling down her cheeks. "I'm sorry. I should've... trusted you. I let those comments get into my head."

"What comments?"

"People saying I didn't deserve you and we'd never end up together or you must be cheating on me because fat girls don't end up with thin, fit guys."

"Fuck that. Fuck all those people and their ridiculous, shameful standards. I've never looked at someone and thought they were ugly based on their physical appearance. What makes people ugly is their soul. The way they treat people. How they view the world. The love in their heart. And you are beautiful in every way." I gesture to my body. "Someday, these abs and—if my father is any indication—about half my hair will be gone. Are you going to love me less?"

She grabs my arm, looking horrified. "Of course not."

The words hang there for a second, and a smile overtakes me. "You just admitted you love me."

She laughs and brushes her thumb over my cheek. "I did. I

love you. And you're crazy if you don't know you've had my heart this whole time."

"And *you* are crazy to ever think I'm stuck with you. I chose you. I'll always choose you. I'll never stop."

"I'm sorry I left."

"I understand. We're still figuring this marriage thing out. It's almost like we need to know each other for more than two months. But if there's one thing I want you to be certain of, it's that I'm your safe place, and if you feel like running, the only place you need to run is to me."

She rests her head on my shoulder. "What about everything else?"

"Like I said, I truly think it'll be okay. But I've already talked to my cousin Stacy about a defamation lawsuit if we need to go there. For now, there's this."

I pull out my phone and open it to the post, the comment section of which has filled up with love and support for us.

She takes it from me and reads through what I wrote, then goes up and scrolls through the pictures, tears spilling down her cheeks as she does.

Then her hand is on my neck and she's staring into my eyes. "I love you."

"I love you too, darlin'."

Her lips land on mine, and everything else fades away. I'm home. In our love, in her, I will always be home.

JADE'S naked body is wrapped around mine as we lie in bed, ignoring the world.

Since that sniveling piece of shit's post yesterday, his world has unraveled. Not only have Jade and I been bolstered with tons of love and support, multiple female authors, influencers, and some fans have stood up and told their stories about Darren Corval. The best thing to see was the bolstering from men in the community who saw some of his predatory behavior and defended women, then spoke up too. Women raising their voices is essential, but men backing them up shows other men that the kind of bullshit Corval tried to get away with will not be tolerated.

He ended up deleting his post about Jade and me.

Stacy was pissed and sent a little cease and desist order his way. It's almost like he knew he was wrong.

I don't know what he thought would happen, but at this point, I don't care.

He's taken up enough of my brain space.

All I care about right now is this.

I graze my fingers over Jade's back, and she sighs happily.

"How would you feel about doing the voice of Jason for the Marianos series?"

My eyebrow quirks up. "Jason, huh?"

"I know you haven't really gotten to see his storyline yet, but he and Evvie have quite the story. And he needs someone with your warmth to voice him."

I stare at her for a long moment. "Would you be willing to voice Evvie?"

She's right, I haven't gotten to see much of their story yet because the book eight cliffhanger ended with a tease of it. I might've gotten a little hyped just reading it. I mean, he's her ex's cousin, her childhood best friend, and she's going to be his nanny. I can't wait for book nine. And damn straight if I'm narrating Jason, I want her narrating Evvie.

She sucks in a breath. "If we both really feel I'm ready, then yes. But I've decided I want to do the series multi-cast. Which means I'd have to be ready soonish. I reached out to some narrators last night."

"Why didn't you tell me?"

"I had to stop thinking and just do it. Plus, I'd connected with a few after everything yesterday, so it seemed natural to start the conversation."

"This is going to be amazing."

"I hope so. Also… I know I kept you busy yesterday afternoon. And last night. And this morning… but you really should check your email."

She gives me a mischievous grin that has me reaching for my phone.

"The first two fairytale books?"

"I'm ready to start pursuing something with them. And who better to read them first than my husband?"

I toss my phone aside and wrap her in my arms. "Say that again."

"My husband."

"Mm, wifey. You have no idea what those words do to me."

"Make you fall a little more in love with me?"

I brush my nose against hers. "Every second of every day. I love you."

"Love you too. Hubby."

That's it. This is my heaven. Nothing like I could've imagined, yet it's everything I want and need. *It's more.*

Getting married in Vegas after knowing someone for less than a month wasn't part of the plan. Wasn't the love story I saw for myself. But sometimes fate gives you the love story you need. Now I'm ready to build a beautiful life with Jade as husband and wife.

CHAPTER THIRTY

TWO WEEKS LATER

Jade

THE END.

Book nine is officially finished. I've reread it and didn't cringe the whole time, which is the best praise I'll ever give myself.

"Hey, wifey. What are you working on?"

Justin binged the first four books of my fantasy series. Now he's begging me to finish the fifth one. I gave him book nine of the Marianos to hold him off, but he reads too damn fast.

"Nothing. Get out of here."

"But I'm desperate for my next fix," he whines.

"And your desperation will only continue if you don't leave me alone and let me finish."

"But why would I leave you alone to finish?" he croons, stalking over to me.

He leans down and grazes his lips over mine, but doesn't deepen the kiss.

And when I open my eyes—since I'd closed them, ready to relax into the kiss—he's looking at my computer screen.

I give him a shove and stand up. "Are you serious right now? Not even three months of marriage and you want my books more than me?"

His eyes fly wide. "No. Never. Literally never. Darlin', you're my real-life love story."

I put my hand to his chest. "Don't you *darlin'* me."

He dramatically falls to his knees. "But baby, I'm sorry. You're just so brilliant. I couldn't help myself."

"Mhm." I turn and walk toward the door of the bedroom, but he chases after me, coming to a stop in front of the door.

"I'm not letting you leave this room thinking I want anything less than every single inch of you."

He steps in, brushing his lips over my neck.

"Oh, really? And who says you're in charge?" I tilt my neck to give him more access, and right when he's let his guard down, I spin around and bolt through the bathroom.

When I spill out into the hallway, he's right on my heels. I squeal when he grabs me by the waist, twisting his hand into my shorts. But that's a mistake because with a shimmy of my hips, the shorts slip down and I jump out of them before he can grab me again.

"You think that's not exactly what I wanted?" he calls.

When I glance back at him, he's stripping his shirt off.

Okay, maybe I get those books where the masked guy chases the girl into the woods now.

I run around the kitchen island, and he skids after me, but the second time I try, he loops back around and we almost collide in the living room.

He crushes his mouth over mine, stealing the squeak I let out.

Pinning me against the couch, he rocks his hips, grinding his hard-on into me.

"So much better than the books."

He slips his fingers inside my underwear, brushing my clit.

"Justin..."

The crack of a loud knock sounds against the door.

Justin throws his head back and groans in frustration. "Nobody's home."

"I'm from WellAlways Insurance Corporation. I need to speak with Justin Ayers and Jade Jackson."

We glance at each other, then down at our clothes. Or lack thereof.

"Stay behind me," Justin says, swinging the door open, but only a crack.

"Mr. Ayers. My name is Rich. I'm an insurance investigator for WellAlways Insurance. I'm here because we received some information that your marriage may have been solely in an attempt to defraud our company into paying for Ms. Jackson's healthcare. Is she available?"

Oh, shit.

Justin turns his head toward me, and I shrug. Not my finest moment, but neither is being accused of insurance fraud.

Justin swings the door open all the way. "She's right here."

The investigator's eyes quickly go back and forth between me and Justin as he takes in my lack of pants, Justin's lack of shirt, and the obvious bulge in the crotch of his shorts.

Justin clears his throat. "We're a little... busy."

"I can see that," the investigator mutters.

"Can we do this some other time? I need a little... time... with my wife."

"Right. Well, based on what I'm witnessing right now, I'm not too concerned about the nature of this citation. We get plenty of false reports. I'll still need to speak to you both and likely a friend or family member who can vouch for each of you. But we can do that over phone or email."

Justin steps back and wraps an arm around me as I try to pull my shirt down. His hand conveniently lands on my ass.

"Trust me, there's nothing to be concerned about here."

The investigator nods, then claps his hands together. "Well,

I'll be in touch. Have fun—ah, a good day. Mr. Ayers. Ms. Jackson."

"Mrs. Ayers," I say coolly, but he doesn't turn back.

Justin closes the door, then turns to look at me, eyes wide.

"Wait. Mrs. Ayers?"

I give a little shrug. I was going to surprise him when my new license came, but why not now?

"Maybe."

He cups my face in his hands, his captivating blue eyes brimming with emotion.

"Did you take my last name?"

"Yes."

"Really?" he rasps, tears welling in his eyes.

"Well, you keep reminding me I'm your wife. I figured it was time to make it official. I want the world to know who I belong to."

He slants his mouth over mine. And like our first kiss, it's so easy to get swept away in it. Just like I was swept up in a whirlwind with him.

He breaks our kiss slowly, staring at me reverently. His breath tickles my lips as he holds me close, like I'm the most precious thing in the world.

"I'm yours," I whisper. "Forever."

EPILOGUE
NINE MONTHS LATER

Jade

I ROLL my shoulders and crack my knuckles.

I'm almost finished with the twelfth and final book of the Marianos series. It's more of a wrap-up novella, and I'm dragging my feet because I'm not ready to finish.

I have a whole new project planned to start soonish. It's all about a group of friends who meet starring in a Broadway show, in their late teens, then it follows them over the next ten years as life starts to imitate art—sometimes a bit too much. It's going to be heart wrenching—and the first series where I'll likely kill off a main character—but I'm hyped for it. And when I pitched it to Justin, he immediately begged me to start writing it.

But I have some other things that need to be done first.

Clicking over to my email, I pull up the motivation to get me through the final edits I'm working on—the cover for my *Beauty and the Beast* retelling.

After I did a thorough edit, I let Zoey and Trish read it, and

Zoey suggested my first query be to the agency she's with for her romantasy series because she knew one of the other agents had been dying for a good fairytale retelling.

That piece of advice made a huge difference for me, and I was a total unicorn and was offered representation from the first agent I queried. If it hadn't been for Zoey mentioning it, I don't know if I would've pitched there right away. Sometimes even the smallest connections make a big difference.

It's been a wild ride, but also a fun one, and it made the time surrounding my healing process fly. I have full hand strength back now, and it's like I never had the surgery at all—minus the fact that I no longer have pain in my hand when I type or do anything else. It's amazing.

With a yawn, I accept that no editing is going to happen until after I've had coffee, so I reach for my ring to put it back on— because sometimes wearing my ring when I'm typing all day drives me nuts—but I don't find it on my desk.

Maybe I left it in the kitchen when I was making lunch.

That's my destination anyway, so I head out of the bedroom, but Justin calls for me from the office, where he's been recording all morning.

I stick my head inside. "Everything okay?"

"Yeah, can you come in here for a minute? I recorded a part today, and I don't know what it is, but I can't get it quite right. Would you give it a listen?"

I shrug and step into the booth. "Sure."

Over the last nine months, we've recorded most of my first interconnected standalone series and we've worked on the first three books of the Mariano Family series so far, though our characters don't have huge roles yet. I've learned a lot about voice acting, and also picked up on Justin's tics when recording, so sometimes he asks me to listen if he's struggling.

He puts my headphones on my head, then steps behind me, out of the way. I push play on the computer and his voice fills my ears. Almost a year of marriage and it still makes me feel all gooey.

I close my eyes as I listen to Justin's melodic voice.

"I know none of this started how we planned, but you're everything to me. I'd be a poorer man without you, living a life devoid of the kind of love you give. I wouldn't trade a second of our life together. Even the hardest days are better because they're with you. You're the love of my life, darlin'."

At that, my eyes snap open. Is that written in a book?

"I'm the luckiest man in the world that I get to be your husband."

Awareness pricks at me, and slowly, I turn around and find Justin on one knee, holding my ring.

He nods toward the headphones, and I pull them off.

"I know we've technically been married for almost a year. That ceremony was beautiful and special, but it wasn't enough. We deserve a wedding that celebrates the love story we've written and the future yet to come. A wedding filled with love and all the important people in our lives. Most of all, I want to stand at the altar and spill my heart out to you. I want to spend all night wrapped in your arms on the dance floor. I want to watch you walk down the aisle in a stunning dress with no questions about what it means or where we're going. So, what do you say, darlin'? Will you marry me again?"

Not a doubt in my mind.

"Absolutely."

He stands up and wraps his arms around me, kissing me as he holds me tightly.

Then he unfurls one arm from around my back and slips my perfect fairytale ring back on my finger.

"This ring means so much to me," I whisper.

"Because it's a representation of our fairytale love story?"

I smile up at him. "Because it was a moment when I realized how much you care for me. You heard a few sentences about how much I loved those stories, and you got me a ring that perfectly fit my dream of being a Disney Princess."

His smile is bright and playful, though heat burns in his gaze.

"I wanted it to be your only wedding. I had to get the details right."

"You got it all right," I whisper. "Especially choosing me."

He laughs and slants his mouth over mine in a passionate kiss.

The truth is, I'm the lucky one. He saw me. He chose me. He did something totally crazy to take care of me. And even though it was scary, I have no regrets.

Our love story might not have been what I thought I'd write, but despite its flaws, it's been a better story than I ever could've imagined.

Thank goodness I said yes when he offered to marry me.

Best decision ever.

The End

Grab a Jade & Justin bonus chapter, check out more of the Baker Girls series, sign up for Bethany's newsletter, and more here:

A NOTE FROM BETHANY

Thank you so much for reading Justin & Jade's story. I loved writing their story and especially Jade's realistic relationship with her body. And I might've been swooning a bit over Justin! I hope you enjoyed it all too.

If you want a romantic scene featuring a much bigger Jade & Justin wedding, you can grab their bonus chapter on my website.

Up next from the Baker Girls is Hallie and Wilson's surprise pregnancy, single dad x nanny rom-com, *The Last Thing*. And if you haven't yet, go back and check out Mark and Frannie's story in *The Last Lie* and Kennedy and Devon's story in *The Last Key*. Plus stay tuned for Hardy and Ackley's story (*The Last Person*).

And if you want to know more about Jade's friends, check out *Finally Yours* (Trish & Mikey) and *Always Mine* (Zoey & Luke).

For more news, updates on what I'm working on, teasers, and freebies, sign up for my newsletter or hop over to my reader group, Bethany Monaco Smith's Book Besties.

Thanks again for reading!

XO,

Bethany

BETHANY'S BOOKS

Freaking Love series
First Love
Real Love
Forever Love

Friends Like This series
Friends Like This
Falling Like This
Broken Like This
Love Like This
Married Like This
(a Friends Like This bonus novella)
Together Like This
Heartbreak Like This
Family Like This
Future Like This
Nothing Like This
Trust Like This
Always Like This

Ida Heartthrobs series
The Forever Fight
The Perfect Love
The Future Play

Baker Girls series
The Last Lie
The Last Key
The Last Love Story
The Last Thing
The Last Person

Ida Romance series
Reckless for You
Faking It for the Holidays
Waiting for Your Heart
(free novella)
Everything for You
Running Back to You
Stealing Your Perfect Heart
(free short story)
Caught Up In Your Love

Lacy Creek series
Finally Yours
Always Mine
Only Ours
Complete Trilogy

Standalone
Fake It Till You Fall
(free novella)
Lost In My Heart
(free short story)

THE LAST LOVE STORY PLAYLIST

You can find *The Last Love Story* playlist on Spotify

- Beauty and the Beast- Leroy Sanchez, Lorea Turner
- A Dream is a Wish Your Heart Makes/So This is Love- Sabrina Carpenter
- Close To You- Gracie Abrams
- In My Dreams- Ruth B.
- Love Story (Taylor's Version)- Taylor Swift
- Beautiful Crazy- Luke Combs
- Speechless- Dan + Shay
- Meant to Be- Bebe Rexha ft, Florida Georgia Line
- Small Town- John Mellencamp
- What's Your Fantasy- Ludacris ft. Shawnna
- Let It Happen- Gracie Abrams
- I Think He Knows- Taylor Swift
- I Could Get Used To This- Becky Hill, WEISS
- You Make It Easy- Jason Aldean
- What It's Like Loving You- Maddie & Tae
- In Case You Didn't Know- Brett Young
- She's Got a Way - Live at the Paradise, Boston, MA - June 1980- Billy Joel

- My Person- Spencer Crandall
- Drowning- Backstreet Boys
- Home- Phillip Phillips
- Long Story Short- Forest Blakk
- Paper Rings- Taylor Swift

ABOUT THE AUTHOR

Bethany Monaco Smith is a writer-mom. When she's not busy hanging with her boys, she's writing beautifully messy love stories.

She loves happily-ever-afters and cries at every emotional moment, whether reading, writing, or watching. When she's not mom-ing or writing, you can find her binge-reading on Kindle Unlimited, supporting fellow indie authors, and having sushi dates with her SIL. Bethany survives on coffee, rewatching the same TV shows over and over, and her KU subscription. She lives in the Southern Tier of NY with her husband and two sons.

For more about Bethany and what she's working on, follow along on Instagram or on her website, bethanymonacosmith.com. Stay in touch by joining Bethany's exclusive Facebook group, Bethany's Book Besties & signing up for her newsletter.

ACKNOWLEDGMENTS

To my right-hand girls Cassie and Lacey, who I couldn't do this without!

To all my fabulous betas for helping reassure me I'm on the right track and swooning over my book boyfriends: Ryan, Stephanie, Melissa, Carissa

To all the amazing authors who support me along the way. I see you and I'm right here cheering you on in return.

And to all of you wonderful readers, I couldn't do this without you. Thanks for being here.